# The Best of Friends

Front cover designed by Robert Sefton

This book is a work of fiction. Names, characters, places and incidents are either a product of the author's imagination or are used fictitiously. Any resemblance to actual people living or dead, events or locales, is entirely coincidental.

*Thanks to my proof readers.*

*As always, Nicola and the kids, love you all.*

Thanks so much for purchasing THE BEST OF FRIENDS and I really hope you enjoy the read. As a bonus, please visit my website www.thomasdunnauthor.com to pick up my **free** novella ANOTHER LIFE. By signing up I agree not to bombard you with spam as some other unscrupulous individuals will do, just information about progress on my writing and new book releases.

**The Best of Friends**

What started as a bunch of friends off for a week of bonding, drinking and generally looking to have a great time has turned into murder, paranoia and potentially the end of lifelong friendships or even worse, their lives.

Can the five friends survive the trip and what will be the repercussions if they do?

## Chapter One

Growing up in Glasgow can be tough. I'm not talking about the new swanky Glasgow that they portray on television now, armadillo's, café culture, bars and restaurants, I'm talking of Glasgow twenty plus years ago. Govan and Ibrox were tough council estates that were decimated through unemployment, drug and alcohol abuse. Everyone has heard of the Gorbals, back in the day, this was an area of tenement blocks and poor social housing were some of the worse standards of living were allowed to fester and grow until they decided enough was enough and demolished the lot.

It's all apartments, shops and businesses now. But if you grew up in Glasgow, the Gorbals had an air of fear about it and unless you lived there, you avoided it. And that still holds true for some people. It was survival of the fittest back then and you needed your friends to watch your back.

I'm not saying Glasgow was worse than any other working class inner city area like Birmingham, Liverpool, Manchester, Newcastle and parts of London, but it tried its best to be. If you lived on one of these council estates, you wore a label which went something like 'scum', 'smackhead' or 'thief', to people from outside the area. Your parents worked at the docks or in factories to make ends meet, these weren't areas of flash cars or two car families, you had your lot in life and you were expected to deal with it.

As a wee boy growing up there, the grassed areas, tenement blocks and shopping parades were your playground and scrapping with other boys or gangs was just part of growing up. My group of friends all lived around my estate and we have been friends since we were knee high. We are a tight group of friends who put up with each other's oddities and are quite happy to take the piss out of each other because of them.

♦ ♦ ♦ ♦ ♦ ♦

I've been friends with Frankie, Razor, Davey and Bobby since we were four years old and we epitomised that friendship, grew up together, got into scrapes together, caused mischief and mayhem wherever we went and backed each other up one hundred percent, no matter what.

Razors name is not Razor obviously, it is his nickname that has stuck with him for years. Razor used to think that we called him that because of his shaggy beard and the lack of shaving, but it's really a bit of a put down due to his lack of razor sharp wit, it took him a while to get onto it!

Razor was born into trouble. His Mum and dad were both alcoholics and he pretty much had to be the parent to his younger brother and sister, Tony and Rosie. We helped him out over the years as best we could. When we were young, we would steal food from our own houses and take it to Razors when we knew his Mum and Dad were out. We thought we were so clever, it was only years later that we realised that our parents all knew what we were doing and even bought extra food so we would have enough to share.

When Razor was eighteen, he got his own flat and moved ten year old Tony and six year old Rosie in with him. His Mum and Dad didn't give a shit about them and social services overlooked his young age and were just glad to get them into a more stable home. Razor didn't get the family allowance book for the kids obviously, that was additional ale money for his mum and dad. When we were all older and had got decent jobs, we would lend him a few quid to help out, he did good by the kids and we wanted to do good by him.

We always loved going to see Razor and the kids, they were always good company when we called around. The kids seemed so happy and barely noticed their Mum and Dad were both missing out of their lives and to be fair, they were never really there anyway. You could always find Mr and Mrs McGregor in the local boozer, pissed up with no intention of spending their hard earned dole on petty things like food, clothes or rent. Never mind luxuries for the younger kids like sweets, pop or presents.

Razors real name is Paul McGregor by the way, but Razor suits him so much better! Razor eventually met Donna (Mrs Razor as she is affectionately known), and she moved in with him, Tony and Rosie and to be honest it was the best thing that could have happened. Donna keeps an organised house, Razor works hard at his landscape gardening, a business he proudly started from scratch. The kids grew up and are still living with them. Razor and Donna have a similar interest in knocking up a joint a few times a night, so all is good and mellow in the household McGregor.

It was tough upbringing for Razor and the kids back then, but to be fair, they weren't the only ones.

♦ ♦ ♦ ♦ ♦ ♦

Davey Donnelly is silent but deadly, just like his farts. But he's the man you want on your side if you find yourself in trouble. Six foot four inches of pure power, no formal training as a fighter, but a beast of a man. I don't know how many times when we were younger when we would get into a bit of a ruck in town and find ourselves outnumbered, we'd all go one on one with someone and Davey would just take the rest regardless of numbers, he is an animal when he gets going.

To be fair to the man, he is a really good guy at heart and wouldn't hesitate to put himself out for you. He's a real gentle giant who adores Razors younger siblings and they love their big uncle Davey.

A few of the lads had tough upbringings and Davey was no different. He was knocked about a bit by his Dad when he was younger until one day, when Davey was about fifteen years old, his Dad was knocking his Mum about and Davey decked him. There was a stunned silence in the kitchen as the implication hit home with Davey, his Mum and then his Dad as to what had just happened.

His Dad left not long after that and Davey's Mum cried and cried. When she stopped crying, she told Davey that they were tears of happiness and she was glad that Davey had become the man of the house. After that, Davey, his Mum Peggy and sister Ann-Maria were a lot happier.

Davey is married to a lovely girl named Mary. It looks quite funny when they are out and about together as Mary is a waif of a girl and only about five foot tall standing next to the man mountain. Davey and Mary have two boys, Tom and Adam and although they are only young, they are nearly as big as their Mum already. They will be at least as big as their Big Da, as they call him. God help the poor boys in school and the neighbourhood if they take after Davey.

♦ ♦ ♦ ♦ ♦ ♦

Frankie McMullen is like the Dad of the group, a big, strong man's man who we all seem to turn to when we need advice or even if we don't need it. If he thinks one of us is being an arse or getting out of line, he isn't afraid of giving a crack around the head. Even Davey, as big and tough as he is, has too much respect for Frankie to argue back.

Frankie was one of us who grew up in a relatively calm household, he is the oldest of five children and his Mum and Dad were both loving parents to the five of them. This sounds too good to be true in our small dysfunctional group, but that's the way it is sometimes. Frankie cruised through school without trying too hard and when he left, got himself an apprenticeship as an electrician and now has a great reputation and earns himself good money. It was later in life where it all went wrong for Frankie McMullen, really wrong.

Frankie lost his wife Maggie to cancer at the tender age of twenty four, they had twin boys Charlie and Jack and he has done a great job bringing them up when he could have completely fallen apart. He was obviously devastated when Maggie died, they'd been together since they were sixteen and were the first serious couple out of the group. Man, they loved it when they were told they were having twins, as were we all, and they both doted on Charlie and Jack.

Frankie had no choice but to keep it together for the kids, they were only two years old. He certainly grew up and in a way it sobered the rest of us up as well. This is the reason that Frankie is so respected. That and his ability to remain calm in a crisis and think things through before he speaks or acts, he calls it the philosophy of 'engaging the brain before you engage the mouth!'

I'd like to think his friends played a part in getting him through his own crisis after Maggie died, it's something that we are proud of as a group of friends, that we've always been around for each other.

♦ ♦ ♦ ♦ ♦ ♦

Then there is Bobby, Bobby Naismith. What can I say about Bobby? He is like a bad smell, lingering for longer than he should. It's quite hard to believe that he is part of this group, when we were at school, he was a spotty geek looking lad who didn't really have any friends. He was usually the butt of someone's joke, sometimes they were quite cruel, but that's kids for you.

It was during one of these 'pranks' in secondary school that involved setting Bobby's shoes on fire, while he was still wearing them, that Frankie made the terrible mistake of stepping in and giving one of the perpetrators a smack. His friends thought they would help him out and piled into Frankie, this was a mistake because even back then, Davey could brawl.

Anyway, wherever we were after that, Bobby would turn up and just...............linger!

Bobby came from a decent family, he was an only child and he had a Mum and Dad who cared for him and gave him pretty much anything he wanted. He told us that he spent a lot of time alone in his bedroom through his formative and early teenage years playing on his computer, games or programming. We all just assumed he was looking at porn, or was that just us? Anyway, he must have been being truthful because when he left school, he set up his own I.T. business and makes a pretty good living from it.

Bobby lives in the city centre in a swanky converted apartment building, he is the only one of us who is still single and he usually has stacks of cash. Yes, maybe we are all a little envious, but he is still a dickhead!
Bobby is just the butt of most of our jokes. He is more of a hanger on as no matter how much of a hard time he gets, it just seems to wash over him.

♦ ♦ ♦ ♦ ♦ ♦

And then there is me, Jack Bonner, I'm probably a mix of them all, except Bobby, *no* one wants to be like Bobby. I didn't have it as tough as Davey or Razor, but I grew up in a single parent household with my Mum, Jean and sister Marie. This was because my Dad just decided to up and off one day because my Mum asked him for a little extra money to get some essentials.

I was four and Marie was three, my Mum ended up working three part time jobs over seven days, so me and Marie spent a lot of time in neighbours, friends or relatives houses. I loved my Mum very much, I didn't quite have the same feelings about my Dad after that.

Apart from the transient lifestyle of living between lots of different houses, we managed to keep our heads up and get on with our lives. We were relatively happy as we were surrounded by a lot of good people and managed to get through school and get some qualifications. I'm a qualified mechanic now and I'm doing okay.

I'm married to a beautiful woman named Nicky and we've got three kids, Sean, Alex and Katie. All is pretty good in our world, we're comfortable with a nice house, couple of cars, and a couple of holidays a year with some beer tokens to spare.

♦ ♦ ♦ ♦ ♦ ♦

And that's the gang; we've been through a lot as individuals and as friends and this has kept us strong as a group. We've had plenty of ups and downs throughout the last twenty or so years, but we've managed to come through them and come through stronger as a result. It always seems as if there is nothing that could tear us apart and if anything or anyone tries, they had better watch out.

## Chapter 2

This trip has been a long time in the planning; we've not been away together since we were about twenty years old. After that, we all seemed to get caught up in relationships, families, mortgages, bills and the rest of the baggage that gets in the way of having the craic with your mates. None of us mind this, kids and family have made all the difference to most of us in one way or another and we value our families more than most due to our backgrounds.

We first started discussing going away over a pint one Friday night. We try and get together about once a month as a group, but there always seems to be one of us who can't make it. Unsurprisingly, Bobby gets there every month, no wife, no kids and plenty of spare cash. Anyway, on one of the few occasions that we did all manage to get there, we were sadly reminiscing over our youth, we're only thirty for God's sake! We got to talking about the last time we all got away together ten years earlier on a week's holiday to Ibiza and what a great time we had and how we should do it again.

We were all young and Frankie was the only one of us in a serious relationship and he was quite laid back while we were away. The rest of us were all pretty manic on the lash and Razor was dropping tablets like there might have been a shortage on the horizon. It was a great time, drinking until stupid o'clock and sleeping late, recovering in some glorious sun and then starting again after some food. Heady days for young men and we had a glorious time.

The more the beer flowed, the more our bravado grew of how we were going to go back and 'tell' our wives and kids that the lads were going back to Ibiza for a tenth anniversary celebration. Well, in the cold light of day, sober and slightly less brave than the previous night, some of us broached it with our nearest and dearest. Words were exchanged and replies to the request like 'how old are you soft arse' and 'you're not a bloody teenager yer know', or 'no problem, I'll pack the kids suitcases for them, they'll love Ibiza!' Let's just say that it didn't go down too well and it got diluted down to something a little closer to home.

We were slightly deflated after this, some mumbling on the phone, a quiet pint to reminisce about when men were real men. Again, it was a good job the wives weren't within hearing distance or our moans would have been met with criticism and disdain.

We were still happy enough to be getting away, we just needed less sun cream. Texts and emails were flying around at lightning speed about where we should go and what type of break it should be. I thought it would be a good idea to go for a nice relaxing spa break, blow off the dust from the daily grind, get some of the oil out of my pores and just generally chill out, the lads just pissed themselves laughing and called me a big tart!

Frankie wanted to go on a golfing break, but as it is only him who plays, no one agreed to that. We all just told him golf spoilt a good walk and he threatened to give us a smack, he's a bit attached to his golf.

As usual, Razor said we should get cheap flights to the 'Dam (Amsterdam to the uninitiated) and get stoned out of our trees and worry about the consequences when we get back. We all laughed and said that would just be a busman's holiday for Razor and the rest of us wanted to hang on to what brain cells we had left. We said that he had lost enough for all of us over the years, Razor just replied that he was the smartest one among us. We all agreed that he was the biggest smart arse around.

Davey said that he would go anywhere were they sold beer and he could maybe have a cheeky scrap with someone, safe in the knowledge that he wouldn't be in Glasgow. He has changed a lot since the 'incident' as we have named that particular episode, but with Davey, some things never change.

Unbelievably, in the end, it was Bobby who came up with the idea that we all agreed with. I could see us all sitting back looking at our laptops or phones thinking 'that's a great idea' and then in the same thought 'I can't believe that dickhead came up with that!' It seems harsh I know, but he is an absolute nightmare sometimes and there is so much less stress when he isn't around which isn't too often.

Bobby has an uncle who has a cabin on a mountainside up in the highlands by Loch Eriboll. Anyone who has ventured that far north into Scotland will have come across some of the most beautiful and unspoilt wilderness in the world and it was agreed that this might just be a great break that could meet all our needs. Plenty of laughs, plenty of beer and a little bit of fresh mountain air to clear away the city cobwebs would do us all wonders.

We all went around to Bobby's apartment one night and he got the area up on Google Earth and displayed it on one of his huge monitors, 'it only cost, blah, blah, blah.....' Once he'd shut up about specification and how much it cost, we all focussed in on the images as he scrolled around the approximate location of the cabin and the surrounding landscape. It looked desolate and there was hardly a house, never mind a village or town for miles around. We sat just staring at the beauty of the place even though it was just a wilderness and I think we were sold on the idea there and then.

And so it was agreed, five guys on a trip to the mountains. We talked about how great it was going to be with no women and no kids taking priority over everything for a whole week, seems like bliss to us all and we can't wait to get going. We might throw in the odd bit of exercise with some strenuous walks, but maybe not, we'll have to wait and see.

So this lodge that we're planning to stay at up in the mountains belongs to an uncle of Bobby. Only for that, I don't think we would have invited him along, he is hard work sometimes. Even sorting this out with his uncle seemed a long and protracted event. In the end I got his uncles number off him and called him to clear a few things up, it was all sorted in fifteen minutes as opposed to the weeks that we had been waiting for Bobby to move his arse.

I don't know what irks more, his bragging about the latest car, furniture, piece of I.T. equipment or the whining voice when he doesn't get his own way. The fact that he couldn't sort this little trip out makes me wonder how he has managed to run his own business for so long and make any money.

There was a real excitement leading up to the trip, we were like a bunch of school kids when we would talk to each other on the phone, email and text. We would say stupid things like only eight more sleeps! How ridiculous, but some of us hadn't been away from the wife and kids for so long, our excitement levels were off the scale. I think Razor had started having sleepless nights he was so excited to be getting away for a week. He said he was going to have to start packing straight away, we think he meant he had to get more drugs.

We met once more for our monthly drink before we went away and firmed up some of the things we would need for the trip. We decided we would do a bit of walking in the mountains, so everyone would have to make sure they had their cold and wet weather gear, rucksacks and spares.  We talked about what kit was in the cabin already, Bobby told us the cabin had a small generator that was just powerful enough to run the lights, all heating and cooking was done with a wood burner and a range. This meant the kitchen and main living space were warm, but the bedrooms and bathroom were cold, so warm sleeping bags would be needed as well.

Eventually the time to leave had come and as much as we were looking forward to it, it was strange saying goodbye to our families the night before, we are all usually together on breaks or holiday, so leaving them feels a little odd.  Like any other couples and families, it is the familiarity of constantly being together that provides the comfort of a home and although this will be a great break with the lads, we will really miss our nearest and dearest.

Frankie has left the kids with his parents, he hates to leave them but he could really do with this break.  There were tears from the twins, but Frankie has promised them Disney in Florida for their holidays next year, but only if they are good for their Ninny and Granddad.  The 'guilt' promises are standard practice for Frankie whenever he goes anywhere, he always ends up spending at least double the cost of the trip on the kids when he gets home.

He doesn't get away that much, just a night or two with work or an overnight jolly with the boys to Edinburgh or down into England.  Liverpool and Manchester are two of the favourite places that we've visited on the lash and sharing our Scottish heritage with the locals.

Tony and Rosie are old enough to look after themselves now, but Razor warns them both about not trashing the house. They have threatened it jokingly, but as Tony now works for Razor and lives under his roof, he could lose his job and accommodation if he misbehaves. Rosie does some part time typing and accounts for Razor while she is at college, so she also has a lot to lose. They both respect Razor way too much anyway to think about messing him around. To be honest, Razor said he was more worried about Donna trashing the place than the kids. That got him a clip around the ear from her followed by a list of expletives!

Davey picks Mary up under the arms and holds her at eye level and tells her he'll see her in a week and not to let the boys walk all over her. He turns to the boys still holding Mary up and tells them that if they misbehave or stress their mammy out, they will have him to answer to. To be honest, if he said that to me, I would do as I was told every minute of every day.

I say goodbye to Nicky and the kids, Katie is the youngest and she cries after me. Nicky says not to worry, they will be okay while I'm away. She tells me to have a nice time and not to worry about anything, just go and relax and come back de-stressed. I promise I will and tell them that we will do something nice together when I get back.

Bobby says goodbye to his computer equipment and furniture.

We are all packed, some of us for the last week and Frankie picked us all up one by one, Bobby last of course! We waved goodbye to our families as we drove off, all sad faces until we turned the corner and then our focus was on the week ahead. This is going to be a fantastic week with the lads, all together for a change as opposed to someone missing due to other commitments. It will be like a year's worth of boozing and laughter rolled into one week, we really can't wait to get to the cabin.

As well as our clothes and walking kit, we pack Frankie's four by four with booze, food, booze, some DVD's, booze, cards, booze, iPod. You get the picture, it's a good job he has a roof rack on the car for the booze or we really might have had to leave Bobby behind. It was that or put the booze in the car and put Bobby in the roof rack, but it's still early days yet, he may still end up there. We set off for what is going to be a great week away, a week of doing anything we feel like without the worry of the wife or kids or the daily grind.

## Chapter 3

We set off out of the city heading north from Glasgow on the M80, if we were doing the drive in one go, it would probably take about seven hours. We've decided to do a couple of pit stops along the way to stretch our legs and maybe have a shandy or two. We can't go mad as Frankie has agreed to drive all the way there and it wouldn't be right for us all to be pissed in the car with him. As we reach the outskirts of the city, we discuss the week ahead and reiterate our desire to have a good time, the mood lightens and the banter commences.

The trip is quite enjoyable and the time in the car goes by quite quickly with a group of friends, good craic and some good music. Although some of the lads just don't have my acquired taste in music and moaned. Razor wanted dance music, this is him continuing to relive his youth although we think he may have spent too much time on E's during his 'rave' days and this has probably made him a bit more bonkers than he really is.

Razor is just a frustrated hippy and always ends a sentence with 'man', 'yeah man', 'do you understand me man' and 'have you seen that man........man!' But he's a good laugh and it's always interesting being in his company.

We drive for the first few hours and the conversations just roll from one subject to the next, sometimes about jobs we've worked recently to maybe something that has happened at home or with the kids, Bobby informs us with some excitement that they have developed a new Pentium processor that is capable of……….yawn. We drive until we see a sign for the Dalwhinnie Distillery which is on the A9 just as it skirts the Cairngorm National Park. September is a great time of year to see the park with the snow-capped hills and mountains of Ben Macdui off in the distance. It is quite a stunning sight to city boys like us and as we get out of the car in the car park, the air is crisp and clear and certainly not the fume filled, grid-locked streets of the city.

After we have parked up at the distillery, well it would be rude not to, we head inside for a couple of wee drams of the hard stuff. To be fair, I think I'm one of the few Scotsmen who don't actually like whiskey, the lads think I'm cracked. The fact that I don't call it amber gold, liquid gold or God's nectar causes derision from the guys, but I just laugh it off thinking who is really bonkers. I don't mind the odd glass now and then, particularly when I'm cold as it can warm you up from the top of your head to tips of your toes.

We spend the best part of an hour at the distillery, sitting on benches in the outside area just enjoying the sunshine, solitude, peace and quiet. The silence is broken by Frankie telling us to get our arses in gear as we've got a good few hours to go yet. We head back to the car and head off, everyone is feeling a little more chilled after the break. Razor and Davey nod off after a few minutes as I think that they had more than a couple of cheeky ones while we were there.

They seemed to take longer than us when they went to the toilet and they certainly went a few times more than was really necessary in such a short space of time. The stupid grins on their face were the real give away though, along with the childish giggling.

As we drive along the A9, which passes through the Cairngorm National Park, we pass through some incredible and beautiful countryside. It is wild and remote and I feel as though we could actually be driving on another planet it is so vast and unspoilt, the views and scenery take my breath away. The white capped hills and mountains look pristine and they cause a glare against the azure sky in the bright sunshine. The many shades of heather and bracken that are interspersed with some wild flower or other draw the eye, as do the vast swathes of pines that line the hills and valleys and hide a multitude of wildlife.

That is the conundrum of Scotland, bright sunshine in one direction, clouds and mist in the other. There are parts of the park in the distance where there seems to be no distinction between the sky and the ground, they just merge into one another with rolling mist creating the illusion of mountains in the sky.

We drive in silence for a while as we lose ourselves in our surroundings, the music plays low, Paul Weller's version of 'Black is the Colour' which feels appropriate as it is based on a traditional Scottish folk song.

The slow melodic tune and rasp of Weller's voice seem to fit in with our surroundings and for the few minutes that it plays, we are lost in the beauty that is Scotland. Sometimes, the ability as a group of friends to sit for a while in silence and enjoy each other's company can be underestimated, but we all know when there are times for a laugh and a joke and times for a bit of peace and quiet. This is definitely one of those times.

After about fifteen minutes of driving in silence listening to some quality music from the IPod, that peace and tranquillity is suddenly broken by Razor who lets off one of the loudest farts you will hear in a confined space and to make things worse, the smell is grotesque. We all open the windows and lean towards the fresh air, Razor gets called all the names under the sun, but we end up laughing along with him, the smelly bastard.

Another hours drive and we pass through Inverness and cross the Kessock Bridge which spans the Moray Firth. The great open expanse of water reminds us that we haven't had a piss for a while and suddenly we are saying to Frankie that he needs to pull over.

Frankie turns off the A9 into North Kessock were there is a small petrol station with toilets; we use the men and women's because we just can't wait! We pick up a few bits while we're at the garage and Frankie tops the car up with petrol and off we go again for the final part of the drive.

After we cross the Cormarty Firth, we take a little detour to what the lads describe as the scotch drinkers paradise, the Glenmorangie distillery on the banks of the Dornoch Firth. We don't stay long, and the lads only pick a couple of bottles each, this is nothing to do with cost, we just haven't got any more room in the car.

Back on the road and back on track, we make good time travelling through this rugged landscape which hypnotises you with its natural beauty. Some of the roads we take are single lane roads that run alongside hills, mountains and lochs that we may never ever see again. We don't need to pull into the lay-bys very often as up in this part of the world, traffic is minimal and the four wheel drive handles the terrain skilfully, even at speed.

The beauty of this great country and the raw remoteness of its desolate landscapes can sometimes be overlooked for sunny beaches or ancient cities. But Scotland and the Highlands and Islands in particular have some of the most exquisite views you will ever come across if you just spend some time exploring them.

We pull over into a layby for a five minute leg stretch and a piss. We are next to some rugged hills abound with pines and heather on one side and some Loch or other on the opposite side. There is not a sound to be heard and it is this tranquillity that I don't believe that you will find in any other part of the world except the most remote.

It is quite breath-taking to stand here with the freshest of country air and some beautiful scenery to match. As we take in the scenery, what I believe is an omen for a good week ahead occurs when Razor points out an Osprey as it swoops down, glides across the surface of the loch and picks a large fish out of the water. We all whoop and cheer when this happens like a bunch of kids, but there can't be too many people who have seen an event like this in real life. Sure, we've all seen something like it on television, but to see such a majestic bird in its natural environment hunt like that was absolutely thrilling.

But, all good things must come to an end and as we watch that wonderful bird fly off into the distance, Frankie tells us to get back in the four wheel drive and it is with some reluctance that we all clamber in.

'No worries boys,' Frankie says, 'there's plenty more of that sort of nature where we are heading.'

Some of us drift off for ten minutes here and there, but Mr Reliable Frankie, keeps his focus and keeps the Jeep heading north to our destination. We're probably about a couple of hours from our destination when we head through the village of Tongue and across the fantastic Kyle of Tongue Causeway, the name is impressive but the causeway is a wonderful piece of architecture and the views are phenomenal.

Frankie wakes Davey and drives slowly over the bridge allowing all of us to enjoy the majestic views and the smells of the ocean. This could be somewhere around where the North Sea becomes the Atlantic Ocean, there is no demarcation, and I'm no expert.

The VW camper van behind us wasn't very impressed with us though, beeping his horn all the way across, I thought those hippy traveller types in those vans were meant to be all mellow and shite. As we reach the end of the causeway, there is a small pull in and Frankie pulls over to let the less than happy camper van driver past, as he pulls past shaking his head, our long-time friendship intuition kicks in and we all give him the middle finger at once.

We are all laughing uncontrollably at our childish behaviour. It made us laugh anyway and it had been a long drive. We pull back onto the road and continue on our journey.

We drive through a place aptly named Hope and are on the final leg of our journey, to be honest, it has been a good laugh and it hasn't seemed too bad being on the road for nearly nine hours. After the euphoria of the first couple of hours had died down, we settled in to our own little conversations, occasionally it would pick up as someone said something stupid or irrelevant and it wasn't just Bobby.

We all took some stick through the journey over one thing or another, but it was just banter between the boys and no one took offence.

We head down the A838 between Loch Hope and Loch Eriboll, this is an absolutely majestic site with these two huge Lochs on either side of us, with rising hills and mountains as a backdrop. The journey continues to throw the most amazing views at us as we draw closer to our destination, at the foot of Loch Eriboll, where it narrows to around twenty metres across, you turn and head back up the other side of the loch and about half a mile along there is a switchback road.

Obviously, we miss the turning for the road because we're not paying attention and ten minutes later we realise that we have missed it and the cussing erupts. Frankie tells us to all shut it and we turn back, heading south towards the foot of the lake.

To be fair, it is no wonder we missed it as it is no more than a small track that switches back in the opposite direction from the road that we are on. This makes it virtually invisible from the road that we are on. We drive along this 'road' and it climbs steadily up the hillside through forested areas that have been planted by the Highland forestry teams.

This road dies out and becomes a shingle track as we crest a rise and see the full glory of the mountain in front. It's not Ben Nevis, but is big enough, its crown is hidden within the low cloud and we get a surge of adrenalin as we head towards our final destination.

Bobby tells us there are only about half a dozen cabins up this track and they are only used during the spring and summer seasons as you can get snowed in for weeks. This happened to his uncle once; fortunately he'd stocked up for a few weeks stay and managed to get out after about a month, Bobby says he got a bit of cabin fever being stuck in there with his wife for twenty four hours a day. He does say that he is surprised that one or the other of them hadn't done away with the other whilst they were trapped.

We head up the track that can only be accessed by a four wheel drive vehicle, it gets steeper and more rugged the further up the mountain we go. We pass some turn offs which we assume are tracks to other cabins, Bobby informs us that his uncle's cabin is the furthest one up the mountain.

It's coming up to five o'clock and some of us are worrying if we will get to it before dark. Some of the bends in the track on the way up have your heart in your mouth as there are no crash barriers to stop you heading right back down the mountain the quick way.

Eventually we see a hand painted sign at the side of the track that tells us we have reached our destination, we head through a small cut in the copse of trees and we reach the cabin. It has been quite a drive and we have a feeling of accomplishment as we reach the cabin, we clap Frankie on the back and tell him what a wonderful job he has done getting us all here in one piece.

## Chapter 4 - Frankie

'I don't know if I can handle Maggie being gone anymore.' Frankie says one night after the funeral. Me, Davey, Razor and Bobby are around at Frankie's house trying to keep his head above the water and keep him from exactly this way of thinking.

'Don't talk like that Frankie, you've got too much still going for you. I can't imagine how hard it must be, God knows man, but you've still got the kids, your family and we're not exactly going anywhere. We'll be here harassing the life out of you until we're on our zimmers and even then, it mightn't stop!' Razor says what we are all thinking, maybe not just the way we say it.

We've all been around to Frankie's most nights together or in ones or twos since the funeral. I don't suppose it's the best idea, but we always bring a crate of beer or three and some bottles of the hard stuff if the beer isn't enough. Things tend to start off okay, but it really is true, in situations like this, drink really can be a depressant. After a few hours, things always end up a bit morose and Frankie is always crying at some point.

We offer to come around of a day when we get some slack and take the kids out to the park or soft play areas to give him a couple of hours to himself or get things in order. He just says no, he isn't letting the kids out of his sight, that he's not losing them. Losing Maggie has cut him to the core and the kids are now his world and all he can think about or so we thought.

Things move on and Frankie pulls himself together and gets back to work. The kids go to Maggie's parents a couple of days a week when they are younger and are not in nursery, which they love as the kids are a reminder of Maggie for them. Frankie's own mum and dad also take care of them when he needs to do some shopping or goes for a pint with us.

We start getting Frankie out a bit to the pub, a bit of hiking or the horses which he seems to be enjoying. Some of us even have a crack at golf which he has always loved, but we give up as it's a bit harder than it looks. We stick to the driving ranges with him after that which is quite a good laugh to be honest, getting to release some of our frustration thwacking golf balls all over the place. It's good to see him back to near normality because we were really worried about him at one point.

Davey had told us that he was on a bit of a pub crawl one night with Frankie by the river and that they were crossing the Finnieston Street Bridge. Davey said that they hadn't had too many, they were a bit wobbly, but not legless and Frankie just stopped at about mid-point of the bridge and looked out across the Clyde.

Davey said it was like he wasn't even there; Frankie just started a conversation with Maggie. 'I can't bear this any longer Maggie, the pain I feel for you, I love the kids so much, but I don't think I can live without you. You were my world princess, you were all

that ever mattered to me, I want to feel you in my arms just once more, but that can't happen and it's all too much to bear.'
It was at this point that Frankie stepped forward and grabbed the railings at the edge of the bridge, his knuckles where white and Davey really thought he was going to throw himself over the edge. He quickly stepped forward and grabbed hold of Frankie in a bear hug 'It's okay pal, it's okay, we'll get through this together, we'll all help you get through this big man.'

Davey pulled him away from the rail and walked him off the bridge with his arm tightly around his shoulders; Davey described it like Frankie was in some sort of trance. They got a taxi in town and headed straight back to Frankie's house, no more beers for them that night.

Getting him out and about without alcohol was part of the plan, hiking, the horses, golf or whatever we could do to get his head screwed back on right, which was all we cared about. And it seemed to work, Frankie was in better spirits wherever we went and he even started to crack some jokes and get in on the banter.

The weight seemed to be lifting off his shoulders, there were still some sombre moments when we were out and about when he would say Maggie loved this place or Maggie loved to have a drink in this place. When this happened, we tried to help him remember it as a positive experience and one he should hold on to.

There was always still an underlying sadness in Frankie, you could see it in his eyes, particularly when we called around for birthdays or barbeques with our wives. You could tell when he started to think about Maggie, he would become withdrawn and you could see his eyes moisten. Our wives spoilt him of course, they would take it in turns to link his arm and talk about the kids and Maggie and you could always tell he enjoyed that.

He hated being away from the kids for too long though and he would never stay overnight anywhere for the first few years. Whenever you called around, he would have Charlie in one arm and Jack in another, they were inseparable and the boys came to rely on their dad so much. This was tough for Frankie, because he had to juggle his work around their nursery and then school; it was a blessing that his and Maggie's parents were so supportive.

Frankie's brothers and sisters live all around the world, one brother in Perth, Australia and one sister in Texas, America. Another sister teaches English to children in Hong Kong and his youngest brother lives in London. They all have their own families and all have busy work schedules, but they all made it home for Maggie's funeral.

Unfortunately, that was about the last he has seen of them since. All except Keith, his youngest brother who lives in London, he gets up a few times a year to see his mum and dad and calls in on Frankie and the kids.

Charlie and Jack both love their uncle Keith very much, particularly as he always seems to bring the best presents with him when he comes up, usually the latest gadgets or magic from Hamley's Toy Store on Regent Street. Keith is doing very well for himself and has managed to get himself a partnership in a small solicitors in London, nothing too prestige, but definitely not one of the ambulance chasing mob. Who says that you can't move up in the world coming from a council estate?

Things for Frankie seemed to settle down into a routine and he managed to hold himself together for the kids' sake if no one else's, but after what Davey told us, we all kept a closer eye on him.

Frankie started going out with Maggie in secondary school when they were both fifteen. Maggie lived a couple of blocks away from Frankie, so they had seen each other around to say hello to and they obviously liked each other. We all obviously thought he was cracked and let him know, although as immature young boys, we all wanted to know how far she would let him go.

Again, to be fair to Frankie, he never told us about what he got up to with Maggie, he was smitten and he even told us that he would marry Maggie someday. We were all a bit shocked, but he said not to worry because he would never stop loving us and then rolled about laughing at us for being such dicks.

When Frankie left school, his dad managed to get him onto an apprenticeship as an electrician for a friend who owned his own firm. Frankie was a very hands on guy at school, woodwork, metalwork and circuit boards where his forte and he picked up electrics very easily.

When the firm went bust during the recession, Frankie didn't dwell on it, he had made enough contacts and friends and set himself up as a self-employed electrician. He managed to pick up some of the contracts that his old firm had lost and went about developing a solid reputation as a reliable and top rate electrician. After that, the work just rolled in, insomuch that he ended up taking on some additional sparks himself and even takes on a the odd apprentice every few years to try and give someone the same chance that he was given.

He also takes on temporary day rate sparks when he takes on a bigger contract than the firm can manage with its current workforce and this allows him to manage some of the bigger contracts that come up. He keeps the business small enough to manage, but large enough to take on the contracts that earn the bigger bucks to keep the business firmly in the black.

I remember when some out of town cowboy outfit was following Frankie around and undercutting him on all the jobs he was pricing for. I call them cowboys as some of the clients were not best pleased when they ended up having to pay twice for a rough arse job that they were left with.

Frankie got wise and started warning potential new clients of what was happening and he would tell them that they would be contacted by this other outfit who would undercut his price. He also gave them the numbers of some of the companies who had suffered at their hands.

After that, firms tended to take notice of Frankie and give him the contracts, this left the cowboy outfit unimpressed. They actually phoned Frankie to arrange a straightener in a car park one Sunday, as this town just wasn't big enough for both firms! Frankie of course phoned us all up and took a couple of his most reliable lads, who weren't bad in a scrap either. It ends up a lot like this in Frankie's game, defending turf and not taking shite from idiots.

Their boss turned out to be a right bruiser who we had heard rumours about, working the doors around the city. We were a little bit worried and Davey said he would take the big fella out. But it didn't bother Frankie at all, he was in the frame of mind to do some damage to whoever thought they could take money from him which meant food off his kids table.

The bruiser had brought about ten of his crew with him and Davey was at his caustic best asking him 'Where are the rest of them yer prick, because if this is all you've got boy, you are in serious fuckin' trouble'.

And that was how it basically went, the fight only lasted about five minutes, but seemed hours with the level of adrenalin flowing. Davey was his usual maniacal self, but it was the first time I'd really seen Frankie in a sort of frenzy. It was like he had lost all sense and he absolutely demolished the bruiser and continued to do so even when he was clearly out of the game. Frankie was on one knee choking the fucker to death, he was actually blue in the face, until a couple of the lads managed to drag him away. He was still trying to kick him in the nuts as he was dragged away from the bruiser's unconscious form.

As some of his crew who weren't lying bleeding on the floor came across to pick him up and throw him in the van, Frankie seemed to zone in and gave a chilling message to the crew. 'If any of you fuckers turn up anywhere near my work or even in Glasgow again, I promise I'll kill you, do you understand, I'll fucking kill you?'

This was the first time we had ever seen this side to Frankie, sure he was a scrapper, we all were, but what he did that day was really frightening. If the lads hadn't dragged him away, I think he might have choked the guy to death.

Davey adds a little extra to Frankie's speech by saying 'Yeah yer pricks, go an' fuck right off!' I don't think this added anything more to the threat, but we all pissed ourselves laughing about it in the pub later. As we all sat there drinking, I would occasionally glance across at Frankie, and I would swear you could still see that rage burning behind his eyes throughout the night.

## Chapter 5

We pull up in front of the cabin which looks a good size from where we are. It is made of log construction and we all look at each other and our faces light up, as if to say that this looks promising. You never know what you're going to get from Bobby; yes, one of his names is Bobby bullshit. Bobby's uncle who owns it has got a bit of money, although no one is quite sure what sort of businessman he is, just that he thinks of himself as a bit of a Tony Soprano.

We park out front and start to unload the kit from the car. Bobby does the 'oh no, I've forgot the keys' thing, no one laughs though, it's been too long a drive. Plus, some of us need a leak and others just want to get the beer in the fridge. It is noticeably colder up the mountain and some of that pretty mist and cloud that we'd seen earlier is starting to roll down the mountain towards us.

Bobby opens up the cabin and when we go inside we are pleasantly surprised. It's a really nice cabin, it's got a big open plan living space and kitchen and four bedrooms, to be honest, we're just happy that it's not a shack and I can see the boys are thinking that this could just work out nicely.

Davey is well impressed, 'This will do nicely,' he says, 'I didn't think it would be as big or as quality as this, this is going to be a good week, I can just tell.'

Yes, there is the downside of four bedrooms and the fact that there are five of us. Guess who drew the short straw and has to share with Bobby the dickhead! The others say it's because I'm the most level headed and seem to be able to manage his whingeing and his mood swings without wanting to punch his lights out. I just think it's because they're a bunch of shites.

Well, I'm certainly not going to let it spoil my break, I plan to make the most of it and enjoy every minute. Sleeping in the same room as someone won't make a bit of difference to the week and hopefully I'll be too pissed to notice.

We work like a well-oiled machine, well almost anyway. Food went in the cupboard, milk, eggs and fresh stuff in the fridge, leaving plenty of room for the beer and liquor. The rest of the beer goes on the front porch, it's cold enough out there now, but it might actually freeze it if were not careful.

Frankie is ever dependable and gets us all outside to bring in some wood from the store at the back of the cabin. Some of it goes onto the porch and he breaks some of it down to kindling and puts it into the large wood burner that sits between the living area and the kitchen. He sets it alight with one of the papers we brought with us and starts adding a few logs to it.

He's like a little boy scout and in no time the fire is throwing out some nice heat and taking the chill and damp out of the room. He carries out the same process with the wood burning stove in the kitchen and we all start to feel the warmth spreading through the cabin. As I look around, I can see everyone is starting to look happier and Razor even starts to sing some unintelligible tune and do an even more ridiculous dance. We all clap along, there's nothing like seeing an old fart dance who thinks he is ten years younger, after a minute, everyone is creased over with laughter and tears streaming down their face.

Razor looks at us all mystified, 'What? What's wrong with you lot?'

We all pull ourselves together and take our kit into our bedrooms doing a half respectable job of unpacking and hanging stuff up, we're not worrying about getting anything creased, as it's not like we'll be out on the town. We all have our own rituals to go through, freshen up, get changed into something 'a little more comfortable' as Razor describes it and generally start to unwind after the long drive.

It's not long before the cards come out, cigars get handed around and lit for those who want one, it's a celebration after all, a celebration of life. A week away from the wife and rug rats and the daily grind of work, you have to celebrate. Davey pours a glass of scotch for everyone and even I take a glass to toast our arrival and what we hope will be a great week.

The beers start to get opened, everyone with their own preferences, Budweiser, Becks, Stella and Guinness are all there and it all tastes good.

Razors brought his usual block of weed with him, when I say usual, this is slightly bigger than usual, about half the size of a house brick. It's not a bad idea to be honest, if we're going to be on top of each other all week, and it keeps everyone a bit chilled, bring it on. Although, to be fair, I think I may need extra if I'm sharing with Bobby!

We laugh and joke our way through the early part of the evening and as happens all the time when you get drunk and stoned, sometimes minor things can bring on the most philosophical debates. It's during one of these nonsensical conversations that I see Davey looking at Bobby as he talks some shite or other and I think I can actually see hate in his eyes.

Davey catches me looking and drops his eyes to his beer, he joins in the conversation as if nothing has happened, but there was something there and I can't quite think why Davey would have such malice towards Bobby. I know he can be an absolute tool sometimes, he has been for years, but we just put up with it and let his nonsense wash over us.

The drinking continues, the music plays loud and the cards come out. We put on some small wagers to try and make it a little bit more interesting and as usual, moneybags Bobby always wants to up the ante and this gets under some peoples skin. Tonight it is Razor, the usually laid back, chilled out, stoned off his trolley one of us.

'For fucks sake Bobby, what is fucking wrong with you? Why have you always got to be showing off, rubbing your money in our faces? Some of us have families and don't have a tonne of spare cash to blow on card games.' Razor is red in the face by the end of this.

'I'm not showing off or trying to rub your faces in it,' Bobby says, 'I just forget, money isn't that important to me.'

Wrong thing to say methinks and here it comes. 'Are you stupid boy?' Frankie erupts. 'Well money is important to the rest of us, we all come from different places to you Bobby, we've all had to graft to get what money we have. You know Razor's been on his arse since he was a kid and he has had to watch every pound and penny he has spent.'

Bobby shakes his head. 'Look I'm sorry alright, I just don't think, it's not meant to wind anyone up. I just got carried away.' His whining voice grates the nerves as much as the words that leave his mouth.

'Just shut the fuck up Bobby.' Frankie says definitively. But I can already see Bobby about to whine some more. Something is needed before the numpty decides to say something else.

'Alright,' I say, 'who wants more beer?'

There is a consensus in the positive, so I get up and get the beers out the fridge and Razor skins a couple of joints, we definitely need to chill out and drop the paranoia. I change the music on the IPod to something a bit more upbeat, too much Pink Floyd can seriously mess with your head after a while. After five minutes, everyone has cooled down enough and the odd joke is thrown in, even Davey is laughing again.

But I see him glancing across at Bobby and it scares me to think of the hatred in Davey's eyes, it reminds me of how his old man used to look.

The evening turns into night and night turns into early morning as we get pissed, high and generally have a good time in each other's company. The earlier issue with Bobby seems to have been forgotten about and he even lightens up himself and cracks a few jokes, this tends to be the way of things, he winds us up, someone kicks off at him and then all is forgotten about, no grudges, no problem.

We sit in the fog of smoke and beer drifting through a variety of feelings from deep, useless conversation to hysterical laughter.

Razor loves to tell us all how many women come on to him when he's doing the gardening or landscaping, particularly at summer when he's in his shorts with his top off, showing off his six pack.

We all groan as it is something we've heard at least a hundred times before, he just brushes us off and tells us all the rich ones where he works are at home bored all day and just want a real man to look after them.

We all roll about laughing and Davey says 'If they want a real man, what the fuck are they coming on to you for?'

Again we laugh ourselves to tears as Razor comes across all indignant and says he could if he wanted, well if he wasn't with Donna anyway, she would castrate him if she even thought he was dipping his wick anywhere else. 'Anyway,' Razor says, 'take a gander at what a real man looks like, man.'

And he proceeds to start taking his top off acting what he thinks is sexily. We all start singing the stripper theme tune and Razor laps it up as he swings his t-shirt around his head and start unbuttoning his trousers.

'Stop it Razor, please.' Frankie begs through laughter, 'Please don't show us your poor excuse for a cock, I couldn't bear the shame of it.' Everyone is now in uproar with laughter, even Razor who falls back on the sofa.

'Yeah Frankie, but you wouldn't want it on the end of your nose as a spot would yer!!' We all start laughing again, and the tears are rolling down our faces. It's probably the drink and weed, but everything at the moment just seems so funny, people are holding their sides in pain we have been laughing so hard.

Things settle down and we start to chat about what everyone is up to and where we see ourselves in ten years' time, will we be looking at another week away with the lads or will we be old, decrepit farts by then. 'Well I won't be sitting in a cabin on the side of a fuckin' mountain with you wankers anyway.' Razor gets the shout out first and this starts us laughing again, less vigorously, but he is so funny sometimes.

The laughter fades and Razor looks at us all sincerely. 'Seriously though boys, me and Donna have been talking about having kids for a while now, Tony and Rosie are older and all that, we need to kick them out and start having some kids of our own.'

We're all a bit stunned by this bit of news and I can see the others waiting for the punchline from him, but it doesn't come. 'What,' he says, 'what, you don't believe I've got it in me or something?' He pulls the funniest faces when he's trying to look hurt or indignant and it raises a smile with a couple of us, but it is half hearted. We can all see that this is a momentous moment in Razor's life and he is opening up honestly to his closest friends.

'No,' Frankie raises his palms to placate him, 'it's just you've never mentioned it before and we thought you were happy enough with the family you have.' We all 'aye' in agreement and nod our confirmations. 'We're all happy for you mate, we will all be there to support you, we'll all be really proud when it happens and I for one would love to be a god-parent to one of the new babies when they come along.'

'Thanks man, I appreciate it, I know I can rely on you all for support. I guess me and Donna will have to curb our enthusiasm around the drugs and stuff, but it will be worth it when we have our own kiddies. We've been a bit jealous of you lot with your kids.' Razor lowers his head as he says this like he is embarrassed or something.

There's silence amongst us as we all think of Razor with a baby or babies and we all feel really good for him. And then Davey throws in, 'That's if you're not a jaffa, yer seedless prick.'

That hand grenade causes an explosion of movement as Razor is on him in a flash, has him in headlock and is punching him to the head and to the body. We all fall about laughing; even Davey can't stop laughing long enough to stop Razor hitting him, leaving him with a split lip. Eventually Razor climbs off him and is laughing along with us.

Razor is breathless and says, 'You're a right arl arse Davey Donnelly, it's a good job you're my mate or I might have had to really hurt you.' We all laugh again because for as long as we have known Davey, no one has ever hurt him regardless of numbers or damage he takes, he is like an unbreakable machine. Except for the once of course, and that was hardly a fair fight.

## Chapter 6 - Davey

Davey Donnelly, what is there to say about this man mountain? He is six foot four inches tall and about what seems three foot wide. Whether he is actually this wide or he just seems that big due in no part to his extreme confidence in his own abilities. His confidence exudes from him and he has an aura about him when he is in yours and other peoples company.

He is a bit like Marmite, you either love him or you hate him, in general, people tend to like him. It is certainly a confidence borne of fearing no man in the city after probably scrapping with some of the toughest of them.

After the debacle of an upbringing, although that is being a little unfair to his mum who always loved him and tried her best to protect him, Davey felt the need to assert himself on other what he termed 'bullies'. This was probably understandable to some degree after the way he was treated by his father and what he saw happening to his mum.

Fortunately, his dad never laid a hand on his sister Ann-Maria, she was a little too young at the time but without doubt, her time would have come though. As Davey put it, 'If he had laid a hand on her, I swear, I would have murdered the bastard'. There is no doubt in any of our minds that even as a fifteen year old boy, Davey would have done it.

There is obviously a bit of a contradiction in what Davey wanted to do in finding bullies and beating the crap out of them. His justification for his behaviour is when we were out as a group or he had gone for a few pints on his own, he would observe the others in the pub or bar and he would be able to pick out the ones who were out for trouble.

He was usually right about it most of the time and it wouldn't take long for him to rattle their cages by glaring across the bar at them or laughing out loud as they passed him. Some say this could be construed as provocation, Davey just explained it as bringing forward the inevitable.

One of the consequences of his crusade that he didn't realise would happen, was that he would also draw attention to himself and attract trouble when he was out. On numerous occasions when we were out, some rough arse or growler type would come into the bar with a couple of his gorilla friends and basically call him out.

Davey's standard reply was to ask them if they wanted to buy him a drink before he beat the shit out of them. They obviously declined in one unpleasant sentence or other and then they would head outside to wait.

Now if Davey was with us as a group, we would always have his back, but we always worried if he was out on his own and no one was there to cover his arse. We needn't have bothered worrying as it was always the same result. After going outside, Davey would walk back into the bar and order a drink with a five or ten pound note that he'd liberated from his 'new friend' for the inconvenience. On odd occasions, the gorilla friends of his opponent would want to get involved when they saw their pal getting a kicking.

But Davey would never rest on his laurels and always anticipated this, always with the same end result. He has had a couple of bottles smashed across his head as well as a baseball bat to no effect, we believe it's because he has a head of granite.

This went on until Davey was about twenty five years old and then stopped. During the years that lead up to it stopping, Davey had defended his title hundreds of times against the 'bullies' as he saw them. To be honest, when Davey came into the pub, it had quite a calming effect, people who were being rowdy calmed down, lads who were arguing suddenly became the best of friends.

Managers and owners of bars would be buying Davey drinks to try and keep him in their bar for as long as possible, such was effect of the big man. As soon as he would leave that bar, the arguments and rowdiness would all start up again unless Davey let people know that the manager or owner had his number and would give him a call at the first sign of trouble.

Davey even had a go at underground fist fighting, needless to say he won all of his fights and he fought some enormous men, strong men and some really good fighters too. But in the end, he was just too good and there was no longer any more money to be made as people wouldn't bet against him. He actually had offers to fight all around the U.K and Europe, but he just laughed and turned them down citing he was 'just a family man'.

Meeting Mary or 'Wee Mary' as he calls her was the best thing that could have happened to Davey. It didn't stop him fighting straight away, but it helped him curb his need to always prove himself. When they got married, Davey looked like a big soft kid in his suit and stupid grin with this tiny doll of a woman stood next to him, but Mary knew how to handle him, talk him down and soothe his temper. This was good to see, because we were worried that he could turn out like his dad, but never once to our knowledge as he ever laid a hand on Mary or the boys.

When Tom and Adam came along eighteen months apart, Davey was ecstatic. We went out after both births and he bought the whole pub drinks all night. He told us having two sons was all he could have wished for and that helped build an even greater bond between Mary and him.

Davey was probably coming to the end of his fighting days by the time the boys were born. But we were out one night in the city centre when a gang of about eight rowdy boys came bustling into the bar, big mouths, flashing the cash, bumping into other customers, threatening them if they back chatted. We were all pretty pissed off with them to be honest, but Davey being the protector of the innocent felt the need to go and have a quiet word with the boys.

He walked purposefully over to the group and we followed a few steps behind. Davey politely asks the boys if they want to settle it down as they are disturbing other customers. Now Davey's size automatically gets people's attention and they tend to listen as did this group of young men. I hear Razor whisper to Frankie 'beak heads' which is the latest slang term for cocaine users.

One of the young men who seems to be the leader of the group stands up in a threatening manner and says to Davey, 'Do you know who the fuck I am pal?'

In his own inimitable way, Davey replies, 'I don't care who you are yer wee little shite, if you don't calm it down, I'll put your head through that fuckin' wall!' At this point, one of the lads sitting to the side of Davey smashes a bottle across the side of Davey's head and the table that they are sitting at erupts as all eight of the boys jump up and start wading into Davey.

We all follow it in but Razor stays on the periphery and is watching as we tear it up with these young lads. All of a sudden, I see him storm into the fight and smash a bottle right across this young lads head which knocks him out cold straight away, Razor reaches down and picks up a large knife that the lad was about to stick into one or more of us.

Davey has wasted four of the lads already and the others are getting a good pasting off the rest of us, they are only boys of about eighteen or nineteen to be fair, so they don't stand a chance. Davey's got hold of the mouthy one and giving him a couple of slaps around the face saying what a hard faced little bastard he is when Frankie says they've had enough. These boys are done, drugs or not, they are out of this fight.

We check that our little group is okay and head out of the bar not a minute to soon as the Police come tearing along the road as we turn around the corner and away from the bar. We are in the clear and head back towards home and to a friendlier boozer where we know we won't get those sorts of jokers in.

It's about two weeks later when Frankie gets a call off Davey to pick him up. Frankie asks Davey where and he tells him at the old paint factory on Renfrew Road by the docks and to be quick about it. Frankie senses there is something not right and picks me and Razor up on the way, we drive through town until we reach the old paint factory just before the Clyde Port site.

We drive on to the vacant plot where we see Davey, sitting slumped against the wall. Even as we drive towards him, we can see he is bleeding from cuts to his head and body and he is cradling one arm with the other. He looks up and he actually smiles at us as we jump up and rush over to him.

'What the fuck has happened Davey, who did this to you man?' Frankie asks, the concern of us all in his question.

'No bother boys, this is all done and dusted, it's all sorted now.' Davey says and were all gobsmacked as to how nonchalant he is being about being on the end of what appears to be a serious kicking.

'Bollocks,' Razor says, 'what do you mean no bother, someone has done you in son and we aren't just gonna let this go!' We all agree that someone needs to be sorted out because of this. But Davey just holds up his good hand, the other looks like it's been broken in several places and is bloodied and black and blue.

'Let's just get me to the hospital and get my hand and ribs looked at and then I'll buy you all a pint and tell you all about it.' And with that said, he gingerly gets to his feet with a little help from Razor and starts moving towards the car, he is clearly struggling to walk and his breathing is ragged. We all clamber in after him and Frankie drives us to the hospital which fortunately for Davey is only about half a mile away.

'To be honest, you could have walked it yer lazy bastard.' Razor throws out and it gets a laugh from us all, even Davey, although he struggles and starts wincing in pain as he does.

'I did try Razor, but I think one of my ribs might have punctured my lung.' Davey wheezes as he talks.

'Fuckin excuses Donnelly, any more of this feeling sorry for yourself and I'll boot you out of this car.' Razor hits the spot and we are all laughing again. Tears stream from Davey's eyes as he laughs and is in pain all at the same time, you've got to love Razor.

Davey gets seen to at the hospital and a few hours later, we are all sitting in our local with Davey bandaged, stitched and stapled. His nose is broken, as well as his jaw and his hand in several places. His lung wasn't pierced fortunately, although it was very close.

One of his five broken ribs was pressing onto his lung which needed some manipulation by way of an incision and forceps to pull the rib away from the lung, Davey took it like a man, but the rest of us watching felt a bit queasy. The hospital wanted to keep him in for monitoring, but Davey was having none of it.

♦ ♦ ♦ ♦ ♦ ♦

'So Rocky, what the hell happened to you and why aren't we getting a team together to get this shite sorted?' Frankie asks. 'We've never seen you with more than a scratch son, you've took some serious damage Davey, how many of them were there?'

'There were four of them.' Davey replies and he smiles as he says it.

'What do you mean four of them?' Razor says and echoes all of our incredulity.

'Exactly what I said, four of them and one of them was an old man and the other was just a boy!' At this we all start talking at once, asking what does he mean a boy, how did he end up like that with only four of them, what's he not telling us.

Davey holds up his good hand and is waving us down as he says, 'Okay, okay yer bellends, let me speak and I'll tell you why this happened, how it happened and why there will be no, I repeat NO repercussions from it.' This brings us all in line and we wait for Davey to carry on and put us out of our misery.

'Right, remember the ruck we got into with those cocaine sniffing shits in town the other week?' We all just nod, no one daring to speak just yet, but all chomping at the bit. 'Well, it turns out the mouthy little weasel was only the son of a prominent 'businessman' aka gangster from over the river. We wouldn't know him, he's top of the food chain and not one of those we know who give the kicking's out to people who step out of line.'

'Anyway, it turns out he was a wee bit upset with the damage his boy received and he found out who I was and met me as I was leaving a job. Nice fella, smart, in his fifties, you can tell he could have a go if he wanted, but there was no threat as he strolled up to me while I was packing the van.

'"Hello Davey" he says and I say hello right back thinking he's a neighbour who wants a job done. "Can I have a quick word with you son", and I say sure, what is it you're after? As I say this a big Mercedes van pulls up alongside us and the side door slides open and in it are two guys who are pointing hand guns at me.'

'Fuck.' We all say at once.

'Yes, fuck indeed,' Davey replies, 'I knew that someone would come looking for me someday, but this old guy was a charmer and he tells me to get into the van and if I try anything stupid, the boys have been told to kill me if necessary. So I'm thinking I won't do anything stupid then. And these guys are good, one sits one end of the van and the other at the far end of the van.'

'The old guy then calmly gets into the front passenger seat and says to me "I believe that you have already met my son", at which point the driver turns around and it is the wee shite from town who turns around still bearing the scars of the kicking he took.'

'Shit.' We say in unison again!

'Ahhh, I say and the old fella says "Yes, ahhh". So now I know I am in deep shit as the old fella explains to me about who he is, the type of 'business' he runs, how he wouldn't usually get involved in this type of thing, but how he was really upset when his son's friends brought him home looking like he'd been hit far too many times by a battering ram.  The old guy is calm as fuck as he says this and smiles all through his chat with me which is scares me more than when I'm angry.'

'He goes on in his calm as fuck manner as to how he had his friends look into my background and found out all about me.  He actually complimented me about how I took care of things and wishes he could of recruited me years ago.'  Davey laughs and winces at the same time, none of us do though, I think most of us are more than a little scared at the moment.

Davey notices us all looking a little worried. 'No worries boys, he knows you just had my back, so he's not looking for any of you.  Anyways, stop shitting yourselves, this is my story.  So we drive across the Clyde and to the old paint factory were you picked me up from and we go around the back.

The old guy gets out and slides the door open and the lads with the guns point the way out, as you can guess, I'm pretty freaked by now but trying to stay calm and look for a way out.'  Davey pauses and takes a long swig of his pint which he almost finishes in one.

We all take this opportunity to take a drink as we are all dry from sitting open mouthed while we listen to Davey talk.  We're not sure which way the story is going to end, the only certainty is Davey got a good kicking.

Davey continues with the story, 'So we're standing there and the son comes around from the driver's side. He's carrying a baseball bat and I'm thinking 'shit!' So the old man says to me how I'm going to stand there while his son knocks shite out of me with the bat and I sure as hell won't retaliate. When the son thinks he has done enough damage, he might let me live, or not. Again, calm with a smile, this guy is seriously scary.'

'His son sets to work on me and although he's swinging it full force and doing some damage, he's a bit of a tart and after about three full on swings, he's getting out of breath. But I'm thinking, I can't let his old man see he's a tosser, so I start groaning and whimpering with each hit and to be fair I think it's working.

That is until his dad stops him and takes the bat from him and he comes over and hits me out of the park a few times in a real frenzy, my jaw and ribs were done at that point. And then as I'm almost out of it, he gets one of his boys to come and hold my hand down and he says maybe this will stop me being such a slugger and batters my hand with the end of the bat, hence multiple broken bones in hand.'

'Just before they leave, and this was the ultimate humiliation, the son comes across and starts slapping me across the face like I did to him and laughing as he does it. I almost laughed as well at the irony but I was in too much pain.

The old man stood in front of me and tells me that he actually likes me and is impressed by my fighting ability, otherwise I'd be dead. Then he said something that stopped me in my tracks and it's the reason why there will be no retribution from me or anyone else. Can you guess what he said boys?'

We all look at Davey and shake our heads. 'No Davey, what did he say to you that would allow him to get away with this. Why will there be no retaliation from you or any of us?' I say what we are all thinking.

'Well the wee old guy has had time to catch his breath and straighten his tie and jacket and who has calmed down again now. He is still being as pleasant as ever, leans down to me and he tells me that I seem a decent enough sort of fella who has got a little out of his depth. He tells me it's time to hang up my gloves and focus on my wife and two children, Mary, Tom and Adam.'

Davey stops and there is silence as we all realise the implication of what the old man has said and the threat to Davey's family if he doesn't get in line. We sit around in stunned silence for a minute contemplating everything Davey has told us and we know we are way out of our depth.

'So then, now Davey's alright, who wants a pint? No harm done hey!' Razor as sharp as a knife as usual breaks the tension and some of us smile at how he manages to do it. But as we look at Davey, we know how close he came to being killed and that it could have been anyone of us. He looks us all in the eye one by one and we see he knows it too.

And that was the end of Davey Donnelly's fighting days.

## Chapter 7

God, I am knackered. We sat up until God knows what time drinking, playing cards, smoking and generally taking the piss out of everything and everyone, but mainly Bobby because he just deserves it. We all drifted off one by one through the early hours, Bobby first fortunately, then me and I heard Razor rattling around in the room next to mine. Davey and Frankie after that, but I'm just guessing as I was well away by then.

I wake up and feel like a bear has been in the room and shat in my mouth, I can barely swallow. I reach for the water on the bedside table, but when I pick it up, it is empty and I just think 'Bobby, you prick!'

The monkey has farted and snored all night, it's been a nightmare. I'd have kicked him out if it wasn't his cabin. It's freezing outside of the blankets and I scramble to get dressed as quickly as possible. The weather seems to have gotten colder overnight; I pull the curtain back and squint with the brightness of day.

There is ice on the outside and it looks freezing out there. Bobby's uncle needs to invest in a bit of central heating up here, I don't know how that will work, he will need a good generator, but it's not even winter and it is already Baltic.

I open the window because the room is rank and close over the curtain, I'm not worried about Bobby waking up, he wasn't worried about me when he was snoring as loud as thunder all night. My breath starts to fog in front of my face and it is icy as I take a deep breath of fresh air. I hear noises from the kitchen and I know it will be Frankie.

Whenever we've been anywhere in the past, Frankie is always first up with the kettle on and a fry up on the go. I think it must be something to do with having to get up with the kids in whatever condition he is in and he never fails them, now he's just looking after the big kids!

I open the door to the bedroom and the delicious aroma of a cooked breakfast fills my senses and starts my stomach rumbling, I can't wait to get something to eat and drink.

I head the toilet, take a leak, wash my face and brush my teeth, I've got a real furry tongue this morning and my breath is skank. It feels like I've eaten some of Bobby's farts they had so much substance! I head out to the kitchen where Frankie has got the range fired up and the wood burner on, it's absolutely lovely in here now. The feeling of warmth after being so cold is luxurious as and I feel the goose bumps recede as I warm up. Frankie acknowledges me with a grunt. 'You want something to eat fella?'

I'm thinking stupid question Frankie, is the Pope catholic, is that bear out there right now taking a dump in the woods?

'Definitely Frankie, I'm starving. Crisps and toast just didn't cut it last night.'
'Yeah, you're right. Someone should of made some food instead of bitching all night about being hungry.'

I know he's talking about Bobby, he moaned all night about being hungry but wouldn't get off his arse and do anything about it. Neither did anyone else to be fair, but at least we weren't whining about it. When you've got the munchies you just want something to eat, you don't want to be standing around cooking. I go to the sink, grab one of the glasses we were using last night and rinse it out.

I fill it with cold water and drink it down in one go, God it feels so good, I've properly got beer dehydration. I fill the glass up again and go and sit back at the table awaiting the veritable feast that I know Frankie is putting together.

Noises start from around the rest of the cabin as people wake up or are just too cold to stay in the bedrooms. It's amazing, I think the smell of a fry up could raise the dead after a session like last night. And by the looks of some of them when they trudge into the kitchen, they look like they have just risen from dead.

Everyone files in one after another with grunts and good mornings or up yours to each other. Bobby is last in and heads straight towards the food, there is not a lot on him, but he can put it away.

'You're a cheeky fucker Bobby, always first at the food, you do the least work and always want to be first at the scran. It's a shame you don't apply that to getting the ale in when we're out in the town.' Says Davey.

'Fuckin hell Davey, it's me letting you stay here, not the other way around. Quit your moanin'!' Bobby is risking Davey's wrath piping up like this. Davey gives him a look like he might just spring across the room and rip Bobby's head off. There is that underlying hatred in Davey's eyes, which again frightens me a little bit because I think he could probably do it too.

Frankie recognises the rise in tension and he cuts in before anyone else can say anything. 'No sweat boys, there's plenty to go around, get stuck in.' He pulls a large serving plate out the oven which has a mound of sausage, bacon and mushrooms on it and puts it in the centre of the large kitchen table, he adds a plate of fried eggs, a pan of beans and a mountain of toast.

There are large pots of tea and coffee on the table already and for the next thirty minutes there is complete silence, except for the sound of chewing and satisfied grunting as we all devour every piece of food on the table.

As we all start to reach our limit, we lean back rubbing our stomachs with satisfaction at what was a genuine feast. We all eat a really good helping but no one can put it away like Davey, but to be fair he is huge and needs a lot of fuel to keep the machine going. You can't beat one of Frankie's fry ups after a session like last night and it really sets you up for the day ahead.

Conversations start up slowly again as we drink the remaining tea and coffee about what the day holds for us. We agree that a brisk walk around the site and through the woods to see if we can get any vantage points and to familiarise ourselves with the terrain of the surrounding area. The plan is that we plan to do nothing too strenuous today, we've got a whole week ahead of us to get some serious walking and climbing done.

After breakfast is finished, we all pay homage to Frankie with a multitude of thanks for his graft at the oven, we are certainly a happier bunch than before we started. A couple of us jump on the dishes and some do the tidying up from the night before, bagging up a tonne of cans and bottles that we demolished and emptying ashtrays. The rubbish gets bagged and put in a storage trailer outside the cabin, this needs to be dropped at the entrance road when you leave.

The usual round of shit, shower and shaves take place, which isn't pleasant after the first couple of people have been in. Fortunately there's a window that can be opened wide in the bathroom that helps. Sitting on the toilet staring at the side of the mountain and listening to birdsong is quite pleasurable and makes a change from frosted glass and the dirty streets of Glasgow.

We all assemble back in the main room when we have sorted ourselves out. Everyone looks better than they did before breakfast and we are ready to get some fresh air. We're not going far, but everyone grabs their backpacks in which we put a few cans of beer, some snacks and a couple of bottles of water. A nice chill out and a few tinnies to quench our thirst later on, as although it's not the warmest day, we are all well wrapped up to face the cold.

We head out of the cabin and Bobby locks up, it seems a bit of a pointless exercise as I don't think you could find this place if you didn't know it was here. Although, there are a wee couple of Glaswegian scumbags I know of who can get inside anywhere. We start having a look around the outside of the cabin, the wood store at the back is full, apparently a local farmer stocks it up a couple of times a year for Bobby's uncle.

The trees immediately around the cabin have been cut back and cleared to create some light for the cabin I imagine. Bobby's uncle has managed to get a large wooden picnic table and benches up here, the type you might see in a country park or somewhere. I ask Bobby about this and he says that the same farmer who provided the wood for the fire actually makes this sort of thing and sells them for miles around.

As you look outwards from the cabin, the canopy of trees that surround it block out a lot of light on the ground beneath them. The area that encircles the cabin seems unnaturally dark for the time of day, almost eerie. A bit of sunshine would help, but we seem to have had the last of it yesterday with low cloud covering the top of the mountain. The temperature is really starting to fall now, it is freezing and the air is pluming in front of our faces as we breathe.

The clouds high above our heads are large and white and Frankie says that there might be snow on the way. We all burst out laughing at once and take the piss out of Frankie the weather forecaster, one of the many other talents he has. He just looks at us and growls and this makes us all laugh harder, he smiles then as if to say 'yer cheeky bastards'.

We spend the next couple of hours wandering around the mountainside not too far from the cabin. We identify a couple of tracks that must be used by walkers and climbers and talk about heading up one or two of them through the week.

We are probably located about a third of a way up the mountain and the cabin is about the last accessible point by vehicle. After this, it is walking or scrambling upwards as the incline increases dramatically. The forest stretches out around the mountain, but thins out the higher up you get and it is past this tree line where we will get the best views across the countryside and the surrounding lochs.

We've been walking for an hour or so now, laterally as opposed to vertically and decide to take a break and sit on an outcrop of rock. From this vantage point we are able to see above the trees and out across the vast wilderness that stretches as far as the eye can see.

On one side we can just make out the stretch of Loch Eriboll in the distance as it stretches out as if reaching to join the sea and on the other is the mountain, its peak surrounded by white rolling cloud. It truly is beautiful country and we are happy to have made the long journey, it almost beats the disappointment of not getting to Ibiza, well almost.

We sit and eat our food and open a can and just listen to the sounds of nature that surrounds us. It's funny as it feels like there is not another living soul for a hundred miles, which is probably not far from the truth. The peace and quiet and the solitude is quite invigorating, the feeling of your own limitations and your potential is inspiring.

The sound of the wind whistling around the mountain, through the trees and across our faces refreshes us as we sit taking in all the magnificence of this vast Scottish wilderness.

Davey finishes his sandwich and stands up at the edge of the outcrop. 'This is the life hey boys, no one demanding your attention, chewing your arse for your latest mistake, *free as a fucking bird!*' Davey shouts the last part out and it seems to stretch out across the sky and fall away down the mountain. We all nod our heads at this in affirmation of the beauty and remoteness of our location.

'I bet this is like how you must feel on your first day out after a long stretch in jail.' Only Razor could come up with an analogy like that. A convict getting out of prison is like being on the side of a mountain feeling as free as a bird. The more I think about it though, the more I agree with him, I must be losing my marbles.

After we finish our second can and water the trees off the bluff, yes we did see who could piss furthest, it's the child in all of us. We start the long walk back to the cabin as we have had enough and have achieved our goal for the day. We also know that we don't have enough supplies to last us for a prolonged stay on the mountainside.

Our thoughts start turning this evenings plans but firstly to whatever we can manage to rustle up for dinner when we get back. We are also starting to run low on water and feeling slightly dehydrated. And as Bobby has drank all his in the first half an hour and is bugging people to share theirs, we decide to make a quick exit or risk throwing Bobby off the bluff just to shut him up.

We get back to the cabin and there is a sense of relief to just kick back and relax. We go through the usual routine and Razor and Davey get some more wood onto the porch for easy access and I help Frankie get the wood burner and the range fired up. We put the kettle on to boil and one by one we head to our rooms to get out of our heavy gear, a couple of the lads lay on their beds and grab a bit of shut eye before the evenings shenanigan's commence.

The rest stay in the main living area having a tea or coffee and unwinding with our feet up. There is some light conversation in the living room and it is nice to just chill out and not have to worry about anything at all. This is turning into a great trip.

The evening goes all according to plan, Frankie and Razor prepare and serve the food tonight, steak pie and chips, because we really know how to live it up. The conversation is easy, with not too many moans and groans and we eat, drink and are reasonably merry for the rest of the night and thankfully, the evening passes without incident. Maybe we are all starting to relax more and no one is taking the bait when they are the butt of a joke, we are all a happy, mellow group.

## Chapter 8 - Razor

Razor doesn't need an excuse for using drugs, but if anyone asks him, he just says 'With an upbringing like mine, who wouldn't take drugs.' That's Razor for you, no excuses, no denial, he lives for the moment and takes it all in his stride.

When Razor first moved into his flat, he had nothing and I mean nothing, not a stick of furniture, not a Knife, fork or spoon. But he was determined to make a success of it for Tony and Rosie, he didn't want them having to stay in that slum a minute longer than was necessary, he'd had to live through that shite and there was no way he was letting the kids go through what he went through.

He was a really great lad as we grew up, which surprised a lot of people who knew his parents and the type of life that he was having. He could of easily have used his upbringing as an excuse to lead a very different type of lifestyle, such as stealing or burglary which a lot of young people did to subsidise their shitty existence. Razor didn't do this and he gained additional respect from adults and his peers for choosing the 'right' path.

There were times when he was younger that he would go for days without anything to eat at all. Mr and Mrs McGregor were your stereotypical coping (sort of) alcoholics. Giro day would come and they would be down the pub splashing the cash with not a thought to putting some food in the cupboards or any decent clothes on Razor.

The first we really knew how serious things were in Razors house was when we were walking home from school one day and Razor just stopped walking, we all carried on for a few steps and then stopped and looked back, The next thing we saw was Razor just falling forward flat on his face .

Being a bit of a joker, we all burst out laughing and saying 'nice one Razor'. But then he just didn't get up and when we went to him, he looked awful. We weren't even sure if he was dead, he looked so pale and his breathing was so shallow, we were pretty scared at the time.

We picked him up and leaned him up against a nearby tree, Frankie gave him a couple of light slaps about the face and we were all calling his name. He came around a bit and I had a bottle of Lucozade, so we poured some into his mouth. He coughed and spluttered a bit, but it seemed to do the trick.

Razor broke down in tears at this point and after a while, he was able to tell us that he hadn't eaten a thing for at least two days because there was no food at all in the cupboards at home. We were only about eight at the time; I only remember this because his younger brother Tony hadn't been born yet thankfully and this really came as a massive shock to us all.

Frankie took Razor home with him where he stayed for a couple of days where Mrs McMullen fed and watered him until he was fit to burst. The scary thing was that Razor's mum and dad didn't even notice that he wasn't at home or just didn't care. He looked a lot better after that and that was when as young boys, we devised a plan to ensure that Razor always had food and drink at home. And of course our parents, unbeknownst to us, were also playing a part in the grand plan that we had hatched.

When Tony and Rosie came along, Mrs McGregor seemed to pull herself together a little bit for a while and she made sure there was a bit of food for the babies, still none for Razor though. When the babies reached about two years old, she pretty much left them to fend for themselves. She seemed to expect Razor to take care of them from then on, which he did admirably. We would invite him around to our houses and he would sometimes bring the babies with him.

Our parents always made a fuss of them and would always leave them well fed, and with a little goody bag of food and toys to take home with them. Our mums would always tell them to keep their food hidden from their mum and dad as if it was a game. It felt like a game of life and death to us, if it hadn't been for Razor, those poor kiddies could have starved to death.

As we got older and became more aware of issues around Razor and the kids like neglect and child cruelty, we started to wonder why our parents never called social services in. Maybe it was because they felt that things weren't done that way around where we lived. Maybe it was the thought that if they did bring social services in, Razor would be sent to a children's home and the babies would go into foster care and that would not help any of them. Or maybe they just had no faith in the services that had already let them down.

It all worked out in the end anyway, particularly when Razor went and got his flat and just moved the kids in with him, it was best move for the three of. Razor had been cutting people's grass, weeding and general garden maintenance for people all around the area from when he was about thirteen to bring in some extra cash into the house. He used this money to buy food for him and the kids, because Mr and Mrs McGregor had no intention of buying it.

He had to be careful and hide his money in new places every week because one time, his dad found his savings and stole it from him and went straight down the pub. It was the one time we saw Razor really lose it, I thought he was going to kill his dad, but his dad was so pissed, he barely even noticed the rage that Razor had displayed.

When he left school at sixteen, Razor had gained some minor qualifications which was quite an achievement considering. But he had made his mind up that gardening was going to be his full time occupation from then on. He was determined to make a success of it and worked really hard. He widened his work area as he could now commit to his business full time. He started working out in the suburbs for bigger houses and richer clients who had bigger gardens and paid a lot more for his work.

He was starting to get a really good reputation and as word spread around the more wealthy neighbourhoods, more and more work came in.

Before that he would put his mower and tools in a wheel barrow and push it to each job, but as work came in further and further afield, Razor found that he needed transport to get himself around. He bought himself a second hand van and got an old guy who lived a couple of doors along from him to drive him around as he didn't have a license yet. He used to give him a tenner a day and old Jimmy was more than happy with this which kept him in 'baccy for his rolly's

Razor passed his driving test first time when he was seventeen, but kept Jimmy on as he had helped him out when he couldn't drive. Jimmy would unload the van, do a bit of weeding and load the van back up again at the end of each job while Razor chatted to the owners and got paid. All the other time, Jimmy would stand around smoking a rolly, rain or shine watching Razor graft.

Razor would work from eight in the morning until at least six in the evening depending on the season and the weather. He would then head home, collect the kids and take them the park, cinema or just for a walk into town, he loved his brother and sister so much and they loved him back with a passion. As they got older and realised the sacrifices that Razor had made for them and was still making, the bond and respect that they had for him just grew stronger.

It got to the point that Razor was earning so much, he had to start declaring his earnings and even got himself an accountant to do his books for him. This was a good move for Razor, he became legitimate, was able to claim tax back on things he never knew about and it is also where he met Donna.

Donna was a clerk in the accountant's office and as she tells it, Razor fell in love with her at first sight. He was smitten though, we could tell it when he was talking about her or when we saw them together. Donna was just as smitten though, Razor isn't a bad looking lad, he is tall and strong from all the manual work without an ounce of fat on him. With his shaggy hair and wispy goatee beard, if he wasn't Razor, it definitely would have been called Shaggy, the character from Scooby-do!

It did take Razor a while to ask Donna out, he later told us he was ashamed of his past at which point we all pissed ourselves laughing. We explained to Razor that he, of all people, had nothing to be ashamed about. What he has lived through and what he had done for Tony and Rosie was nothing short of miraculous, in fact he was a bit of a hero to us all. When we told Donna this one night, she took Razor into her arms and cried telling him 'he was a big soft shite and she would of loved him whatever his past'.

After that, life was a bit of a party for Razor and Donna, they spent a lot of time in clubs, smoking weed, dropping tablets of one sort or another. But Razor always took care of Tony and

Rosie and never missed a day's work through his clubbing lifestyle and of course we always saw him regularly. We were also his clients and whenever he came around to sort our gardens out, we would always have the craic with him. There was also the monthly get together where we would share our latest news or just take the piss out of each other.

There was only ever one concern that we ever knew about with Razor and that was when I'd been out for a drink with a few people from work and was heading home at around midnight. I'd had a few drinks and as I was walking down one of the backroads in town I thought I saw Razor up ahead of me, I increased my pace to try and catch up with him, but he is a lanky string of piss and was easily outpacing me.

He turned around a corner ahead of me and I carried on walking to the corner which led to a bit of an alleyway, under one of the lights just inside the alley, I saw Razor handing over some money to a dealer. I called out to Razor as he took a packet of something from the dealer and they both looked like they had been caught by the Police. Razor came striding towards me looking mightily pissed off.

'What the fuck are you doing here?' He snarled at me, gone was the laid back loveable Razor that we knew and he had been replaced by one who looked like he had a bag of heroin in his hand and wasn't happy with anyone knowing about it.

'What the fuck are you doing Razor, since when have you ever been messing around with that shite?' I'm shocked at seeing him with heroin, I know he'd dappled in most things, but surely he wasn't doing smack.

'It's got fuck all to do with you Jack.' He spat back at me. 'Me and Donna are just experimenting, that's all.' And with that, he skulked off in the direction from where we came. I wasn't sure what to do or say, should I tell the others about it? I sure as hell didn't want one of my lifelong friends becoming a smackhead, but I didn't want him to think I was grassing him up to the others.

I decided to let things go for the time being and the next time we met for one of our monthly sessions, he just gave me a nod when he first came in. Later on when I went for a leak, Razor followed me to the toilets.

'Are you alright Jack?' Razor asks me.

'I'm okay Razor, what about you?'

'I'm good yer nobhead, don't worry about the other thing, it was just a little tester to see what the fuss is about, it was good but not good enough for me and Donna to go full hit on it.' And with that, the discussion ended. I still kept a look out for Razor and any signs that he was heading down a dangerous path with heroin. But true to his word, it did just seem like a phase he went through and there was never any evidence that he was addicted or a regular user. He was just Razor, back on the weed, laid back, bonkers but funny.

## Chapter 9

For the next couple of days we get into a routine of sleeping a little later, all except Frankie of course, eating of which bobby always seems to be first in line and relaxing. There is no television reception up here, but Bobby's uncle has a television and DVD player and we watch some of the films we have brought up.

We have a rule of no porn wherever we go, Davey says it's too tempting and he doesn't want to walk in on anybody having a sly wank, he looks directly at Bobby when he says this. There is no phone and no mobile phones, due to no signal, and no internet. This means we are all lost without our technology, it's like losing one of your senses, it has just become a natural part of your day to reach for your phone. You can see everyone checking their phone for signals one by one throughout the day 'just in case'.

We go for short walks in either ones, twos or as a group just to blow the cobwebs off and get some fresh air. It hasn't got any warmer and I think Frankie might be right about the snow, there is the occasional light dusting which seems to be a prelude of what is to come.

On the fourth morning, we get up early having all gone to bed a little earlier and get ourselves prepared for the day ahead. We've all agreed to go for a good walk up the 'big hill' as Razor calls it. Bobby whines as usual and gets shut up by a number of us, he says he just wants to stay in the cabin and watch a DVD, or he has a bad leg, ankle, back, etc., etc.

'Get your arse in gear Bobby, we've got a few more days left of this break and if you're going to carry on like a big girl, I might just tie you to a tree and leave you for the bears or wolves or whatever's out there.' I say to him. He is not happy, but is wise enough to shut up.

We all go back to our rooms and get our thermals on, outer layers and walking boots. 'I wish you would cut the whining out Bobby, it's the main thing that gets on the lads nerves about you.' I say to him but feel like I'm talking to a brick wall.

'I don't whine Jack, they all just get on my case the first thing I say and label it whining!' Bobby's replies never fail to amaze me. I find it difficult to talk to Bobby when he is in this type of denial, why doesn't he see what an absolute arse he can be sometimes?

'Like saying; 'I'm hungry or I'm starving or I'm really hungry' a hundred times through the evening isn't moaning. Not once did you get up and make some food, just sitting on your arse until Davey got up and made some toast to shut you up?' I'm starting to lose my temper with him so I grab the rest of my gear and head out to the living room.

We check we have got drinks, food, a map and compass for our hike as well as a few other emergency rations and matches just in case. We get our boots on at the door and load our packs onto our backs and head out into the great outdoors.

The morning is freezing, but we are well wrapped up against the cold. Frankie and Davey set a good pace sticking to the well-worn trails that we have seen over the last few days. Me and Razor follow closely behind and guess what, Bobby is trailing behind already.

As we move up the mountain, the trail becomes non-existent and we are taking a circuitous route up the mountain as some parts are too steep or just sheer rock face that we can't get up. The trees have thinned out and as we move forward we are building a bit of sweat now as the day warms slightly and our exertions start to tell. If Bobby says 'can we stop' or 'can we slow down a bit' one more time, I am seriously contemplating throwing him off the next ledge we come to.

To be fair, I think he's really starting to struggle now. He is a skinny bugger, but I think sitting in front of a computer every day and virtually no exercise is really telling on him now. He is red in the face and sweat is rolling down from his hairline. I tell him to take his very expensive coat and hat off to help with the sweating, but as usual he just ignores me.

We push on regardless of the moaning and after about two hours, we take a break for some water and a bit of food. Frankie's sausage and bacon butties go down great and the water is helping with the rehydration. We're all catching our breath, but Bobby is snuffling like a pig, we all seem to notice this at the same time and laughter erupts from us all. All except

Bobby of course, who's got no idea of what we're laughing at? As we sit around, the cacophony of birdsong and other animal sounds surrounds us and we all take it in turn to point out different species that we recognise. It really is exhilarating to be getting a bit of exercise and plenty of fresh air after basically drinking more than our body weight in alcohol.

It is really cold up on the mountain as we eat and drink and our fingers really feel the cold with our gloves off, I can feel them tingling as the cold takes hold. The air seems a lot thinner and with the effort we are expending, we are all getting a little out of breath.

After our rest stop, we push up higher into the mountain, there is a lot more scrambling up as opposed to the steep traversing that we did in the first couple of hours and a few of us are starting to feel the effects of last night. I think Bobby is on the verge of collapse and I'm worried he'll have an accident, I don't care that much, but some of us will have to carry him down if he seriously injures himself. Or we could just leave him?

After another couple of hours, I ask the other lads if it time to start heading back as it's around two o'clock and I don't want to get stuck up here in this weather. It's turned really cold and there's the first fluttering of large snowflakes in the air. It's all very pretty, but if there is a heavy snowfall it will make the descent a lot more difficult.

After a quick discussion we all agree that we should head back and we make a quick stop for fifteen minutes to grab some food and drink before we start heading back the way we came. As we make our way down the mountain, the cloud catches us up and the mist envelops us. After about an hour walking and everything looking the same, Frankie calls us to a halt and looks around.

'I don't know how we've managed it, but we have come off track and I can't seem to get my bearings.' To be fair, we're back amongst the trees and with the mist thickening and the snow falling, we can't make out any landmarks around us. It's also hard to see anything with the thick cloud obscuring the sun and because we've been finding the easiest route up, we've not been travelling in one single direction.

Everyone laughs, we all think Frankie has a built in Satnav system, regardless of where we are or however pissed we are, Frankie can always be relied upon to get us home. On this occasion, we can see that he really is lost. We all turn to Bobby who pulled the rations, compass and map duty.

'What?' Bobby says, I can already hear the defensiveness in his whining voice, I can tell something is not right.

'What do you think, we're lost and you've got the map and compass.' Razor says to him.

'I haven't got the map and compass, I picked up the rations, I thought someone else was getting them.' A hint of desperation edges his words as he realises he has fucked up big time.
'Are you serious, it's the only thing you were asked to bring yer dickhead?' Davey pipes in, exasperation clearly evident in his voice.

'Why was it down to me to bring, I can't even read a map or use a compass, why the fuck would I bring them?' He's starting to whine now and it's like the scraping of chalk being dragged down a blackboard.

We haven't even got our mobile phones with us which would be useless anyway, the reception is non-existent, but there might have been something this high up. But I suppose that was part of the attraction of coming out here, a bit of peace, quiet and isolation.

Frankie's voice booms out 'You're a fucking retard Bobby, you can't do anything fucking right.' With that, Frankie starts heading down the mountain, it's too cold to stay stationary for too long.

We all glare at Bobby and have to double time to catch him up because Frankie's on a mission and nothing can stop him once he goes off on one.

We walk for a couple of hours without stopping in a general downward direction and we're all feeling the pace, we've hardly shared more than a couple of words in all that time. The light is fading fast, the temperature is really dropping and we are all starting to get a bit twitchy about where we are and the possibility of getting stuck on the side of the mountain.

Frankie comes to a stop and looks around. 'I've got no idea where we are and I'm not sure if we are going to get back tonight.' His voice is solemn when he speaks, which means the situation is quite serious. We always know when there is trouble ahead, we recognise each other's serious tone of voice and when we need to listen.

I speak next because I'm the one least likely to get my head bitten off. 'Do we need to think about setting up some sort of shelter and get a fire going before it gets too dark?'

Frankie, Razor and Davey look at each other and Davey growls. 'That's probably not a bad idea, we haven't got much light and if we don't do something, we might freeze to death.' At least we have the cover of the trees here, if we get to the bottom of the mountain and find ourselves stuck in the open, which really might cause us some problems.

We have some shelter from the wind and the snow, but not completely and we have access to wood for a fire here as well.

We divvy up the jobs of firewood collection and shelter making, I take Bobby out to collect firewood whilst the rest of them gather materials to make a bivouac. I want to keep him as far away from the lads as possible right at the moment so he can't antagonise them anymore. By the time we got back to the camp, the lads had started on constructing the bivouac and were doing a great job of it, so we dumped the firewood close to the entrance and I stayed to get the fire started while Bobby goes out to get more wood.

'Don't get lost now.' Razor shouts after him, 'Tosser' added under his breath. The boys all start chuckling and I'm sure Bobby can hear them as they aren't exactly subtle when they are laughing. I feel bad for him, the lads can be caustic sometimes but he really does bring it on himself when he does things like this.

The fire is going so I head out to get more wood and I suppose to make sure Bobby 'numb nuts' really doesn't get lost. Back in my scouting days, finding a large log to put next to the fire helped keep the fire going all night by sheltering the fire and burning the log slowly. I find one and give Bobby a shout to help me drag it, I might as well have not bothered, it was like dragging it on my own.

We get back to camp and the bivouac is almost complete, they've made it between two trees situated close together and used some rope to tie a branch between the two trees and then broken branches off surrounding trees to make the lean to. They have then covered the branches in leaves and sods of dirt to try and keep any snow out and keep a bit of heat in.

We place the log almost on top of the fire and then add a few more branches to keep it going and head out for the last time to gather some more firewood, it's almost dark now. We bring the wood we've collected and drop it on the substantial pile that is there, we know we will need it all.

It's quiet and tense in the camp, but we have got some food and water, so we won't starve, but we may freeze. It wasn't warm to start with, but it must have dropped another ten to fifteen degrees since it went dark.

The bivouac and fire are doing their job and we are warm and dry, thankfully it is not raining and we are keeping our fingers crossed it stays that way. The snow isn't falling too heavily at the moment so there is no danger of it putting the fire out, but we decide to take turns to stay awake to keep the fire going to make sure we stay as warm as possible.

We sit quietly lost in our own thoughts looking out into the night. We keep the fire well stocked and the heat it is throwing off is keeping us all comfortably warm. We are thankful for small mercies and try to keep focussed on how we will get back to the cabin in the morning.

In the dark the snow continues to fall and the cloud and mist swirl around the camp creating shadows and ghosts that seem to be dancing around us.

'Listen,' Frankie breaks the tension 'let's put this behind us, keep warm and stay positive. Things will look better in the morning, I'm sure of it.' Frankie being the adult amongst us again but we all remain silent. I can see Davey is still seething but Razor just shrugs and puts his hands out to the fire to warm them up.

I just think to myself how could Bobby have been so stupid to leave the map and compass, it's like he does these things to provoke the lads, almost like he means it.

The fire crackles and the silence on the mountain weighs heavily on our shoulders. No one speaks, it's as if the person who speaks first could open an avalanche of hate directed at Bobby. Maybe it's best this way.

Frankie takes first watch, razor second, Bobby third, Davey and then me. All is seemingly fine until we are woken by shouting and screaming, everyone jumps up and Davey and Bobby are missing. Its pitch black as the fire has died off to almost nothing, just embers and the log glowing red.

We all run off to where the shouting is coming from. We recognise that it is Davey's voice and when we get to where he is, he has got Bobby by the throat up against a tree. He has lifted him completely off his feet with one hand and Bobby's feet are swinging and kicking in the air. 'You little prick, how could you let the fire go out, we could all fucking freeze to death up here, what the fuck is wrong with you?' Davey screams and spittle flies into Bobby's face.

Frankie and Razor step in and get hold of Davey and try and get him to let go of Bobby's throat as he is gurgling and turning blue, even in the dark. There is no other sound on the mountain and the shouting echoes across the vast space.

'Come on Davey, let him go, this isn't helping anything.' Frankie shouts at Davey and the sound of his voice seems to have the desired effect. There would be no way of them getting him off Bobby otherwise. Davey has completely lost it at this point and we can all see that he wants to do Bobby some real harm now.

Bobby falls to the ground gasping and struggling to catch his breath and I go to him to make sure he is ok, although I could strangle him myself.

'What were you thinking of stupid? Why did you let the fire die off?' I ask him.

Bobby looks up at me and he is just about getting his breath back. 'I didn't let it die, I threw some wood on it and went out to get some more. I needed a dump while I was out here and when I finished I was heading back with it when this maniac jumped me. He could have fucking killed me, he's mental.'

We both look towards Davey who is stood with Razor and Frankie and he does have a murderous look in his eyes. This is always the fear with Davey, the violent streak that he has and the thought that he has more in common with his Dad than we would care to admit.

'He's full of shit, he didn't have any wood when I grabbed him.' Davey says and steps forward towards Bobby. Frankie grabs his arm to stop him, Davey just shrugs him off but turns away anyway, he is sucking in big gulps of air as he tries his hardest to control his temper.

'I was just starting to collect it, I couldn't see anything because it's so dark. Come on guys, why the fuck would I let the fire go out, I don't want to freeze to death?' He looks to each of us individually as he pleads his case. To be honest what he is saying is true, if he lets the fire go out he would freeze as well and I think the penny drops for all of us.

'Let's just get back to the fire and get it going again, it's fucking freezing out here.' Razor may be a bit dim, but that's the best suggestion I've heard all night.

We all head back to the camp picking up wood as we go, Bobby was right, it is dark and quite hard to find wood on the floor. Frankie gets the fire roaring again and it's good to feel the warmth from it. The wood crackles as it burns and as our adrenalin levels drop, it feels as cold as ever.

Nobody sleeps for the rest of the night and the conversation is muted. Every now and again someone gets up and goes to gather wood, even Bobby goes out again followed by glares and muttering from the group. There's no craic and no laughter, just glaring at Bobby who looks like he could cry right about now.

## Chapter 10 - Bobby

Bobby Naismith a bit of a geek, a bit of a hanger on and a BIG pain in the arse for all of the lads. To be fair, if Bobby wasn't about, we wouldn't have anyone to take the piss out of all the time, he does get a proper roasting sometimes.

I'm not sure how to describe Bobby really, his life is a bit of a parody sometimes, he is one of the gang through his own force of nature, but he does everything in his power to balls things up or drive us mad with his constant moaning or whining. And if it isn't enough that we have to put up with that, he is absolutely loaded and wears all the best kit, Hugo Boss, Armani, Lacoste, Pretty Green, Paul Smith, you name it, he has it.

He has all the latest technology, fifty inch television, surround sound, 3-D, bells and whistles. He has the latest IPhone the minute it is released, basically anything he can spend a fortune on, he does and he likes to talk about it constantly in our company until somebody tells him to shut his cake-hole!

To be fair, he hasn't had it all that easy. He was an only child and his mum and dad did spoil him and overprotect him, which is why he sounds like a spoilt brat when he goes full on into whining mode. He always had technology when he was younger, his mum and dad bought him what he asked for, so it was no wonder that this was where he developed his skills as he moved through school and into adulthood.

When we were in school, Bobby turned out to be smarter than the I.T. teacher at our secondary school. He would show him different network products and development and would also be able show him different programming languages that he was working on.

The teacher didn't have a clue of what he was talking about. Bobby self-taught himself computer programming and has done a remarkable job whilst doing it, he was certainly the most computer savvy kid in our school.

He left school with a mix of qualifications but excelled with his I.T. and gained an A star in his GCSE. We all assumed that he would go to college and then university to improve himself in his programming and whatever else that geeks do.

But Bobby had other plans. He started writing apps and programmes for different companies that he knew about and had researched and developed things he knew they would be interested in. Give the lad his due, he is obsessively focussed around computers and certainly knows his stuff.

So much so, that he had earned a whole raft of money before his seventeenth birthday and decided that he needed to get his own space where he could develop his I.T. company further. With his mum and dads support and some of his own money, Bobby put a deposit on the city centre apartment that he now lives in, a two bedroomed loft apartment that at the time cost £220,000.00. We were all thinking that we should have stuck closer to him at school and picked up some of the I.T. skills Bobby had.

He ended up buying the apartment outright a couple of years later for cash, that's the sort of money he was pulling in. There is talk of him being a millionaire, but I'm sure he would have told us about it plenty of times if he actually was, but he can't be far off.

We've all been to the apartment, not too often though, sometimes he becomes a little too boastful of his achievements and you want to throw him off his 'south facing balcony'.

He has divided his substantial living room into two parts and has the living and kitchen area at one end of the apartment and he has his work area at the opposite end. This is to ensure that no steam or cooking smells can penetrate his beloved equipment. He talks with such affection about his tech', a bit like the rest of us talk about our kids.

His workspace is like a cross between the TARDIS and the bridge of the Star Ship Enterprise. It is really impressive to see, with all the cables, monitors, servers and laptops everywhere. He actually had a company build a specialised one off air conditioning unit that takes the heat from the main pieces of equipment and vents it out of the apartment keeping all of the equipment cool.

He obviously had to tell us all about it, particularly as he helped design it and part owns the patent on it. To be fair, he could have told us it can fly to the moon, we had given up listening at some point when he started to get technical.

So Bobby works hard and is a bit of a genius. But he can still be hurt as we all witnessed when both his parents died when they were on holiday in Thailand in 2004 when the tsunami hit. Bobby hid his emotions very well and went about sorting transportation home and the funerals like a piece of business, he said he needed to think of it like this or he wouldn't have been able to cope.

It felt cold and detached, but he had to fly out to Thailand, identify his parent's bodies, get them home and sort the funerals as he has no other siblings for support. He told us it was absolute chaos out there at the time with hordes of grieving people searching for loved ones in amongst the dead and dying. Bobby was 'lucky' that his parents were in an exclusive resort and their bodies were recovered quickly.

This was one of the times we all tried to pull together for Bobby, he may be a pain, but we still considered him as one of us. To be honest, this just involved us all calling around for a few nights, bringing beer and food and playing on his games consoles which is one of his favourite pastimes after his programming. He appreciated the support but promised us he was doing fine, but we knew he wasn't himself as his bitching and moaning was virtually non-existent.

After the funeral, we all went for a few drinks and Bobby talked about his mum and dad and how they had doted on him and that he had them to thank for all his success in business as they had supported him with his interests in computing. He said he was selling their house up in Pollockshields. His mum and dad lived in a beautiful sandstone detached house in Albert Drive and it was worth a few quid I can tell you that.

Bobby was obviously the sole benefactor to his parents will and he got the house and their savings which were 'substantial' he told us. We all groaned inward at the thought of him getting more money, it's true what they say then, money goes to money.

On the upside to Bobby, when we were younger and would get in the odd scrap or two, he would always get involved. He would be last in to the melee, but he would have a go when he was in there, I suppose adrenalin will do that for you. But to be fair he was always there when it went off and like the rest of us, he never backed down.

There is something about Bobby that is cold and calculating in the way that he goes about his business and personal life, like he is detached from his feelings sometimes. When we have the craic, he laughs along, but you look at him and he seems not to be fully appreciating the joke, maybe that's because he is usually on the receiving end of them.

But he must be happy enough, because he has the money to move on and have other like-minded 'geek' friends if he wanted. They could all sit around and talk technical 'stuff' to their hearts content and I'm sure he wouldn't be on the receiving end quite so much.

I've only ever seen Bobby lose his temper once though when we were having a night out for someone's birthday. We were in a club in town and he had had a few too many when a group of lads started taking the piss, pushing and shoving. We were a little separated from each other and I think Davey was having a slash, but Bobby found himself surrounded by a few of these lads and it was starting to turn a bit nasty.

I turned and give Frankie and Razor a shout and turned back to move towards Bobby who had one of these lads stood nose to nose with him, shouting in his face properly trying to intimidate him. I knew then that it was about to go off, the lad clearly thought Bobby was on his own and would be an easy mark for a kicking.

As I got to the edge of the group, I see Bobby scream in the lads face and then I see his arm come up swinging in a wide arc and smash a bottle of beer across the lads face. The place erupted as all this lads friends steamed into Bobby, it all happened so fast that I could barely keep up with it. I moved in and started pulling lads off him and Frankie and Razor jumped into the melee.

I can still recall vividly Bobby with an animal like expression on his face getting punched from all angles, but still trying to give as good as he got. When we waded in, the lads lost a bit of their resolve. A few seconds later, the massive form of Davey comes crashing in like a bowling ball for a strike, punches and bodies flying everywhere.

Frankie pulls me and Razor out and I see Davey grab hold of Bobby and we all start to head for the exit. We can see the door staff moving across the floor and we take a circuitous route avoiding them as we swiftly exit the club. It was a struggle to avoid them as Bobby was screaming and shouting that he wanted get back at the bastards. He was red in the face, veins were protruding in his neck and spittle was flying as he screamed his obscenities.

'Calm the fuck down there wee man.' Davey says to him and gives him a firm slap across the face. A firm slap off Davey is like a good punch off someone else, but it seems to have the desired effect as Bobby lets us guide him out of the front door of the club and onto a rain drenched street.

We all certainly had a lot more respect for Bobby after that, he knew he had no back up and was outnumbered, but he took the fight to them and wasn't afraid of the consequences. It was certainly unexpected, particularly the ferocity and savagery that Bobby displayed that night.

The next day, I called around to see him at his apartment, he was lying on the sofa with a big bottle of energy drink next to him and a bag of frozen peas on his head. His face was covered in bumps and bruises, but he couldn't remember a thing that had happened. All he could remember clearly was being carried by someone and it raining at some point.

He accused Razor of spiking his drink as he seemed to have no idea of anything after a certain point in the night, so I fill him in on most of the pertinent details. He laughs to himself, although at the moment, this is too painful for him so he slides groaning further down the sofa trying to bury himself in the plush cushions.

After a couple of minutes of sitting in silence and wondering why I had called around, I grab my coat and start for the door as it looks like he is fast asleep. 'Jack.' Bobby calls after me, 'Did I really do okay last night?'

"Yes Bobby, you did okay mate, you did more than okay.'

'Thanks Jack, thanks for coming around as well, you're a real pal.'

I leave the apartment and step out onto the street and into the sunshine and think that I am his friend, regardless of the nuisance value he can cause, I am probably his only friend.

## Chapter 11

We are all awake at first light, the cold and the numbness in our bodies means it takes us a while to get the blood circulating to our extremities and warm us up. We stand around clapping our gloved hands together and stamping our feet, it looks a little ridiculous, but it is so cold right now.

Razor has piled the remaining wood onto the fire to try and warm us all up before we go on our way. The snow has continued to fall all night, not heavy at this point but certainly steady and there is a good layer on the floor between the breaks in the trees where the branches don't reach.

We eat and drink the last of our supplies and head out in a more lateral direction as Frankie reckons we are probably not too far above the height that the cabin is located, he seems more certain of himself in the clear light of day. It is also a lot clearer now with the cloud and mist having withdrawn back up the mountain.

He says we must just have got turned around somewhere along the line and we have were probably travelling in the wrong direction last night. After an hour or so, Frankie suddenly changes direction as if he's known where he was going all along and in less than thirty minutes we are in sight of the cabin.

There is a palpable release of tension and stress that has been building up for the last hour and everyone gets a spring in their step, even Bobby.

When we reach the cabin, Frankie sends me and Bobby to get more wood from around the back of the cabin. We bring some around form the wood store, put some of it on the porch and then we carry wood inside from the porch into the cabin where

Frankie is getting the wood burner and the range going. People are tired and angry after a sleepless, restless and uncomfortable night and head off to their beds. I stay in the living room on one of the sofas with Bobby on the other.

Bobby gets up and puts the kettle on to boil; this in itself surprises me because he generally does fuck all when we are away. Another shock is that he gets mugs out for everyone and starts to brew up, this is definitely a first. He wanders around the bedrooms handing out coffee without a word and then comes back into the living area and sits down.

'I'm so sorry, I really didn't think the compass and map were down to me and I definitely didn't let the fire die off on purpose. But Davey's reaction was way over the top, I really think he would have killed me if you guys hadn't come along.' Bobby says in his nasally way.

'Just forget it I say, everyone is a bit too stressed right now, just let it go.' I really don't want to talk about it right now, I'm exhausted from head to toe and through to my core.

We sit in silence for a while, just glad to be back in the safety of the cabin and feeling the heat envelop the room. The warmth from the wood heater and Aga seeps through me, thawing out first my extremities and then deep into me and I feel myself starting to drift off into a deep slumber brought on by exhaustion.

I dream of the mountain and being lost and of something malevolent hiding in the dark, this really scares me and I'm not sure why.

I don't know how long I am asleep, but I'm awoken by knocking on the front door. I'm confused, dazed and all over the place and I have no idea of the time as I drag myself off the sofa and stagger across to the front door, rubbing my face to try and wake myself up. Bobby doesn't even flinch as I reach the front door, but there's nothing new there as he has never liked to exert himself.

I'm still groggy when I open the door and squint as my eyes are assailed by the brightness of day, there is a man in some sort of uniform standing on the porch. 'Good afternoon Sir,' he says slightly too sprightly for my mood, 'my name's Robert Page and I'm a Ranger for the National Parks Team, I'm wondering if I could come in and have a quick word with you?'

'Yeah, sure come in.' I walk ahead and the Ranger follows me inside, stamping his feet and shaking the snow from his coat and closes the door behind him. 'Take a seat, do you want a coffee?' 'Yes please, just a quick one before I have to head on.' He takes his leather gloves off and stuffs them in his coat pocket and then hangs his coat on a hook on the back of the door.

He sits on one of the chairs at the kitchen table as I make some fresh coffee and looks around, he barely notices Bobby. To be fair Bobby hasn't even stirred and the Ranger is probably wondering why he is asleep in the middle of the day.

'I'm just wondering how many of you are up here and how long you are here for?' the Ranger asks me, there is no suspicion, just like he is after information.

I walk over and hand him his coffee and put some sugar and a spoon in front of him. 'There are five of us, but the rest are in the bedrooms. We've had a bit of a rough night.' I then proceed to tell him about our hike and the trials and tribulations of our night on the mountain and this is the reason we are all asleep in the middle of the day.

I shiver as I recall the details and the fear I felt at being lost and possibly stranded up there. I also recall the dream that haunted my sleep and the fear I felt of the darkness and what it was hiding.

'Wow, you guys were so lucky. That's what I've come to talk with you about, there's a storm blowing in from the north-east and it's going to be huge. If it had been tonight you were out, I think I would have been collecting your bodies at the weekend!' That scares the hell out of me, the thought that twenty four hours later if we had got stuck on the mountain, we would all be dead.

The Ranger continues. 'You can see the front it's already started outside, but we are expecting massive snow drifts and high winds, so my advice is if you don't have supplies to get you through to the next week or so, I would think about making your way home now.'

I ponder what the Ranger has said and I think to myself that that this is about right after last night's debacle. 'Well that's put an end to our trip then, is the forecast accurate, it's definitely going to be today?'

'Well it's as accurate as any forecast we can give. The Met. Office are never usually too far out with their forecasts, especially for this region with walkers and climbers out and about. But if it doesn't happen, don't think about taking us to court, we have to give you the option.' He laughs at this, drains his coffee and then stands and heads towards the door.

'I've got one more cabin to call in at about a mile back down the road, I think they must be out on the mountain, but they usually don't stray too far from the cabin. Mr and Mrs Douglas are regulars who just like the solitude of the mountain. After that, I'll be heading back to base for a wee dram of something to keep me warm through the storm. I hope to be seeing you guys again in better weather next time.' The Ranger says as he finishes fastening his coat.

'Yeah, me too. Thanks for the warning; I'm sure we'll be heading off soon.' As he opens the door, I can't believe how heavy the snow has started coming down in the fifteen minutes that he has been here.

The snow is even thicker on the ground and the wind is really whipping the snow around the cabin now. I'm just thankful that we won't be stuck on the mountain tonight. We say goodbye and I close the door after him and walk back into the room. Bobby stirs from his slumber and asks what's happening, I tell him what the Ranger has told me and he just shrugs his shoulders in disappointment.

I head off to the bedrooms to wake the guys and give them the bad news. They are all in a foul mood, mainly due to lack of sleep and I get the usual responses of 'for fucks sake' or 'you've got to be kidding me'. As if things couldn't have got any worse, we've now got to head home early. I head back to the kitchen and put the kettle on, get some clean mugs together and ten minutes later we are all sitting in the living room discussing options.

Razor comes up with his usual answer of 'Let's grab a cheap flight and head to the 'Dam.' Frankie says he doesn't fancy that, but what about a few nights in a luxury hotel somewhere with a swimming pool and sauna and this gets general agreement. I think to myself that I suggested this before we came to the cabin and got laughed out of the pub for it, but Frankie's the daddy obviously.

Looking out of the window, the snow is coming down really heavily and the wind is becoming ferocious and blowing it in all directions. I suggest staying and waiting it out, we have enough food and supplies to get us through to the weekend and beyond.

This gets a few grunts and an odd 'not with our luck' and so the decision is made to head back towards home, but stop in a nice hotel for two or three nights, get some sleep, some good food and beer and a bit of chill out. We all head to our rooms and start to pack our kit together, Frankie goes out and backs the four by four up to the porch and opens the tail gate. When he comes back in, he is covered from head to toe in snow and has clearly struggled getting to and from the car.

'Jesus, it is wild out there, I can't believe it's turned bad so quickly.' We all look towards the windows and we can see that we need to get a move on. The snow is now thick on the ground and is covering the branches on the pine and fir trees. Visibility is poor and the howling of the wind warns us of worse to come.

♦ ♦ ♦ ♦ ♦ ♦ ♦

Just as we are finishing packing up, we hear the noise of a vehicle pull up outside. Davey heads to the door and opens it just as the Ranger is coming up onto the porch, the Ranger pauses when he sees the size of Davey but Davey just steps aside in a welcoming gesture and the Ranger stamps his feet on the porch to shake the snow off his boots and enters the cabin.

The gusting wind blows in after the Ranger followed by a swirling of snowflakes, Davey has to use his considerable strength to force the door shut again.

'Hey guys, how are you doing?  I'm really sorry about this, but the storm has hit a little quicker than we expected and took down some trees along the track and the snow is drifting against them, we're blocked in up here.'  Groans around the cabin gave him our feelings on the matter.

'I guess we're stuck with your idea then, we're staying in the cabin for the rest of the week.'  Frankie spits out as he glares at me.

'Well, thankfully we've got enough food and beer to get us through; we could have really been in the shit otherwise.'  Davey adds and doesn't seem too put out by the news.

'I've been trying to radio in, but can't get through to base, there's too much interference just now. I'll keep trying the radio, but I might have better luck with it tomorrow when the worst of the storm has blown over, I just need to let them know I'm safe so they're not risking lives with a search party. I hope you've got enough room for one more?' The Ranger asks.

'Of course, no problem.' A couple of us respond at once. The Ranger smiles and starts untying his boots and we all head back to the sofas and chairs and sit down.

'How long do the storms up here usually last?' I ask.

'There's no real way to tell, but from experience, they blow in hard for twenty four hours and then settle down for another twenty four and then they start to clear. You guys should be able to get out of here in three or four days. If worse comes to worse and we can't drive out, I can radio in for them to come and collect us or even airlift us off the mountain if necessary.' The Ranger tells us, hoping to reassure us about the process.

'Nothing else for it then,' Razor chirps up, 'beer o'clock methinks, who's having one?' There is laughter around the cabin at last, and Razor being as chilled as he is, always knows how to break the tension with a joke or stupid comment.

We've all developed a bit of a thirst all of a sudden, even the Ranger. And so, the first round of drinks hit the table and then continue to flow that way for the next few hours. The mood lightens as the beer flowed and the wise cracks started to roll off the tongue as well as the piss taking. And yes, Bobby got it in the neck as usual, this seemed to cheer everyone up, even the Robbie the Ranger joins in.

It turns into quite a good evening, Robbie is a good laugh and tells us he is actually from a place called Lossiemouth which is just under a couple of hours drive from Inverness. He tells us it is a nice little place, but has an RAF base up there which tends to cause a bit of consternation with the locals due to the noise of the jets or the 'fucking English' who can't help getting pissed up and causing ructions.

We all laugh when Davey says that it sounds a great place for him to move to and crack some English heads together. Robbie says he will make the right introductions as Davey would be welcomed and very popular up there for that! We spend the next fifteen minutes bashing the RAF, the English and anything at all relating to England, including the national anthem, meat and two vegetables, the Queen and all the other scroungers in the royal family…………..and of course, the RAF at Lossiemouth, even if some of them are Scots!

As the storm rages on outside, the wind howling and thick flakes of snow fall, time passes quickly and everyone seems to be relaxing again. Every now and again someone looks out of the window and says 'Jesus' or 'Christ' as they see the ferocity of the storm, it's amazing how you become all religious at times like these.

Even through the double glazing you can clearly hear the howling of the storm, the creaking fabric of the building as the wind buffets against it. The wind rushing through the trees creates a ghostly sound that makes us glad to be locked down in the cabin. The fire crackles and we are all warm from the heat of the log burner and the alcohol flowing through our system.

There is even less angst towards Bobby who looks like even he might be enjoying himself a little bit at least. As the night draws to a close, one by one, people started heading to their rooms for some shut eye. Surprisingly, Frankie and then Davey were the first to turn in, which left me, Razor, Bobby and the Ranger continuing with the drinking.

Bobby followed soon after and then it was my turn, I was feeling very drunk and suffering from the previous night's lack of sleep. You have to know when you've had enough with these boys, because you know you've got more of the same the next day and the day after that. It's a marathon, not a sprint as Razor likes to remind us all.

## Chapter 12 - Jack

Me. Sensible Jack Bonner, steady Jack Bonner, calm, steady, reliable, wonderful Jack Bonner. The lads have called me all of these things over the years...........okay, maybe not wonderful and maybe a few uncomplimentary names as well. Compared to the others, I think I'm pretty well rounded, not too many dramas to worry about and I am quite happy in my lot.

Growing up was difficult, there were always money problems in our house, the not enough money kind. My dad was unskilled labour and was in and out of work all the time, this made it a struggle to get into any kind of routine in terms of buying food, clothes or other essentials. Not having money made dad angry, but not in a violent way, he just used to brood a lot and wanted to be left alone.

As a young boy who just wanted to spend time with his dad, I found this difficult, particularly being told to piss off all the time. Now I'm older, I think he may have had some sort of mental health problem such as being bi-polar because of the extreme mood swings that he displayed. When times were good they were very good, but when the work and money dried up, they were grim.

When he eventually left, it was a storm in a teacup really, quite literally. We had run out of milk as my mum had been trying to stretch the housekeeping as much as she could and hadn't enough to get some fresh milk. He had been back in work a few weeks, but we were still struggling after him being out of work for a couple of months catching up on rent arrears and other debts. That was when mum asked him for a bit extra to get a few essentials. It was like an explosion as he burst out the chair, red in the face calling her all the names under the sun.

Me and Marie were only kids and we cowered back in our seats and as I say, my dad wasn't a violent man and this was the first real time we had seen him lose his rag like this.

By the time he had stormed out of the room and out of the front door, my mum was a bag of nerves and tears streamed down her face. Marie went to her first and then I did to give her a hug and some comforting words which at our age weren't much as we were so upset ourselves.

I tried to make her smile by telling her I would make her a nice cup of tea, but we had no milk. She gave an anguished smile but could not hide her sadness and she hung her head so her hair would cover her face and hide her tears.

The next few days we spent in limbo waiting for dad to come home, but he never did. He left with the clothes on his back never to return again. I'm not sure what happened to him after that, thinking of his depressions, I wouldn't be surprised if he went and threw himself in the Clyde. We heard nothing at all from him after he left.

Mum got as much work as possible and we spent our early years travelling to and from anyone who would have us. Once we reached our teens, mum was happy to leave us for a few hours when she went out. I got a Saturday job at the garage where I still work, cleaning, sweeping, putting tools away, making tea and answering the phone. Marie got a Saturday job in a hairdressers doing all the dogsbody jobs in there.

We both used to split our money with mum, we did offer it all, but she refused to take it and ensured that we treated ourselves with the remainder. It wasn't much, but just having a few quid in our pockets in our early teenage years was great. To be fair, she always got a chippy tea in on a Friday which was when we handed our money over, so she was giving us some of our money back anyway. We never got a chippy tea when dad was at home.

I've always been around for the lads when we have had problems and tried my best to help them out as best as I can. I'm not the greatest scrapper like Davey and Frankie, but I always have a go, I like to describe myself as a 'lover not a fighter', this always raises a laugh amongst the boys, I've no idea why!

Whilst I worked weekends and holidays at the garage, the manager Marty used to show me the ins and outs of what it takes to be a mechanic and I tried my best to take it all in. By the time I reach sixteen years old, I have a good grasp of engines and the running of a car and know my way around the garage and its tools. Marty is a good guy and offered me an apprenticeship, I was absolutely ecstatic, as were my mum and Marie.

The money wasn't great, but Marty knows my situation and throws an extra twenty quid in each week as part of his 'bonus' scheme for urchins as he regularly referred to me. He is a big guy who demands hard work from his lads, but he earns respect for being an honest and supportive boss.

I am certainly happy to go the extra mile for him for what he has done for me, he has even been lenient when I've come in a bit worse for wear after a night out with the lads.

Marie worked in a solicitor's office as a clerk when she first left school and we used to carry on giving mum half our money from our weeks wages. We agreed to do this as long as we were at home as we were of a mind that she had sacrificed everything for us, working three jobs to keep a roof over our head, food in our stomachs and clothes on our back. She even supported Razor, Tony and Rosie as best she could when they were younger and had nothing and Razor adores my mum for what she did.

Sometimes the boys would pick me up from work on a Friday night and Marty would invite them in for a brew, this usually meant a couple of beers or scotch that he always keeps in his office. He thought a lot of the lads and would always tell me to stick with them and I would be alright, I fully intend to, they are a great bunch of lads.

I finished my apprenticeship and Marty offered me a full time job, which again I accepted without hesitation, I think loyalty is a rare commodity and it's what me and the boys have with each other.

I was working in the garage when Nicky my future wife brought her car in for a service. She got out of the car and I just thought 'Hello, I think I might fancy you a bit', that was all in my head of course, what actually came out of my mouth as a stammer was, 'Hhhhelllo, cccan I help you?' and blushed ridiculously. I'm not sure what happened, in my head I thought I was a bit of a charmer, but the connection between my brain and my tongue seemed to malfunction at the worst possible time.

Nicky just smiled shyly, seeming to understand my discomfort and told me she had brought her car in for a service. I managed to pull myself together and have a reasonable conversation with her, explaining the process of the service and when the car would be ready, we then moved on to where she was from and school and what she did for work. I was impressed that she had her own car and seemed independent and before she left, I asked if she fancied getting together and going for a drink. To my astonishment she actually said yes.

We went for a drink the following weekend and hit it off. We arranged to meet again on the Sunday for a drive out somewhere and have something to eat and spend a few hours together. Things go better than I expect and it seems that she really likes me as well and we are a little inseparable for the next few weeks.

When I turn up for a few beers one Friday night with the lads, they all took the piss for the rest of the night singing love songs to me, the wedding march, imitating cupid firing his bow and all the other stupid things that boys do. To be fair, everyone got the same treatment when they met a girl who they were smitten with.

Me and Nicky settled down into a comfortable relationship and after a couple of years of going out together, we buy a little house that needs a bit of work doing to it and move in. Six months later, we book a weekend away in Edinburgh and while we are having a lovely meal in a bit of an upmarket restaurant, I propose to her. After she stops crying, she says yes and we are married six months after that.

She gets pregnant right away and nine months later we have our first child, a baby boy who we call Sean. It is the best experience of my life and I cry like a bit of a baby myself. Alex comes along twelve months after Sean and Katie follows twelve months after Alex. We are overjoyed with the kids and although three kids in three years is more than we could have wished for, they are all healthy and all seem happy although they are very hard work.

Nicky is delighted with the children as she is a qualified nursery nurse and has always loved being around kiddies. All her family have been really supportive and love their grandkids who add to their already growing family. Nicky is one of four sisters and she seemed to have set a trend as two of her sisters got pregnant after Sean came along, lots of cousins for the kids to play with as they grow up.

Nanna Jean and Aunty Marie are also overjoyed with their new family members, Nicky included, who gets on so well with them. But Nanny Jeans' grand kids are the apple of her eye and a couple of years later, Marie and her boyfriend have their first baby, a lovely little girl called Grace who loves her older cousins. Me and Marie have talked often of never leaving our families the way dad did and to always support each other through any difficulties that we encounter.

The boys are all well pleased for me and as usual, they all want to be Godparents to the kids as each one comes along. This is clearly a difficult decision for me as although I would always pick Frankie, Davie and Razor as Godparents, I also feel a little bit sorry for Bobby, because no one has ever picked him for the job. When I talk to the lads this one night about the dilemma, they all just tell me to get a grip of myself.

They say to think about what it actually means to be a Godparent and that if anything happened to me and Nicky, the Godparent would be responsible for that child's wellbeing both in life and spiritually. They ask would I really want this responsibility to fall to Bobby, who is a fucking imbecile and that it may be contagious and he may pass it on to his Godchildren! This gets a good laugh from us all, it's a good job Bobby isn't around, I'm sure his feelings would have been hurt at this.

I still feel some guilt around this, but regardless, Frankie and Davey are Godfathers to Sean and Alex and when Katie comes along, I actually pick Bobby to be Godfather. I speak to Razor about it first and he says he understands but hopes I die a slow and painful death and poor Katie doesn't pay for my stupidity.

I thank him for his honesty and when I speak with Bobby that night, he is absolutely overjoyed that I have chosen him and promises to be the best Godparent around. I warn him that he can't spoil Katie and if he buys her a present, he has to buy them all a present otherwise there will be hell to pay. He agrees and true to his word, he buys them all presents at the christening which helps to keep a happy equilibrium in the Bonner household, but not in the Razor household.

I have no tales to tell of fighting multiple enemies or heroic acts of saving my friends, I'd like to think that I am just Mr Reliable and always around for them when they need me, whatever the trouble. Even for Bobby.

## Chapter 13

I wake up the next morning feeling only slightly better than I did the day before, I feel like I had a really restless sleep and haven't managed to get all the rest I needed, strange dreams disturbing my usual unconscious slumber.

The traditional sounds were coming from the kitchen as usual; and again the wonderful smells of a cooked breakfast filtering around the cabin assail your senses and I feel my mouth salivating in anticipation. I quickly get dressed, take a leak, throw some water on my face and head out to the living room where Razor is crashed on one of the sofas and Frankie is busying himself making drinks and breakfast. He throws a mug of coffee down on the worktop for me.

'There you go.' He says. He seems uncharacteristically in a foul mood, I'm assuming he didn't sleep well either. He is usually quite cheerful in the mornings or maybe it just seems that way as he is always up before us and we are all grumpy as hell.

I head over to the Kitchen area and get the coffee. 'Cheers.' I say, trying to keep the conversation upbeat, 'That was a decent session last night, but I'm shattered this morning.'

'Aye,' Frankie says, thawing slightly, 'what did you do with the Ranger, is he in Razors room?' Frankie asks.

'I don't know. I went to bed and left him and Razor drinking. I assume he must be, he can't be outside can he?' Frankie stops what he's doing and looks at me as if to say 'Are you stupid boy!'

Davey comes out of his room and comes into the kitchen and says 'Without fail.' I assume he's referring to Frankie's ability to get up wherever he is and cook breakfast. We both grab a plate off the rack and pile our plates up with eggs, bacon, sausage, beans and toast and head to the kitchen table.

Bobby stumbles into the living room next. Surprisingly, no one really speaks with him and then Razor is stretching and groaning as he wakes up. He heads towards his room, disappears for a minute and then is back out and heads for the breakfast.

When Razor and Frankie have filled their plates, Frankie asks Razor, 'How's your boyfriend?' He gives a small chuckle as he says it.

'What are you talking about?' Razor replies, he is clearly baffled by Frankie's question.

'Robert the Ranger, he is in your bed after all!' Frankie says laughing out loud now.

'He's not in my bed mate, are you sure he's not in yours?' Razor sniggers as he shoves a fork full of breakfast in his mouth.

'He's not in mine sunshine; I can assure you of that. Is anyone going to own up to having Robert the Randy Ranger in their bed?' Everyone bursts out laughing at this and after a few seconds everyone settles down again.

'Seriously though, where's the Ranger?' Frankie says and everyone looks at each other with blank expressions. 'Come on boys, someone must know where the fuck he is. Razor, go and check your room again, maybe he's sleeping on the floor or something?' There is an edge to Frankie's voice that wasn't there a minute ago.

'Oh for fucks sake, I'm trying to eat my breakfast. I wouldn't mind, I've been completely out of it on the sofa all night!' Razor gets up with his plate and is still shovelling food in his mouth as he heads to his room.

While Razor heads to his room, Davey goes to the window and looks outside. 'Well, his jeeps still there, so he didn't go anywhere in that. It's buried in about three foot of snow anyway.'

There's some noise and a bit of crashing and banging from Razors room and then some noises and screams. Razor sticks his head out of the door and just as he is about to say something, a hand reaches across his face and he starts screaming. 'Get off Randy Robert, I'm not blowing it again!!' We all fall about in fits of laughter, there is only Razor who could do what he did. He comes out of the bedroom with an empty plate and the fork sticking out of his mouth and a big smile on his face. 'Nope, he's not in there.' Razor says and people's laughter starts to die off as it starts to dawn on us that the Ranger doesn't seem to be in the cabin.

'Bobby, go and check the other rooms.' Frankie says.

'Why me?' Bobby says, but before he can say another word, Frankie roars at him.

'Because I've just told you to you little prick!' Frankie seems to explode.

We're all a little shocked at Frankie's outburst and the room goes quiet. Thankfully, Bobby appreciates the situation and gets up quickly and heads to the bedrooms. We all wait in silence looking at each other across the room.

Bobby comes back into the room. 'He's not in any of the rooms or the bathroom.'

We all look towards Frankie. He looks worried and heads over to the front door, unlocks it and opens it up. The wind is not as wild as it was last night but is still blustery and it blows in snow that has accumulated on the porch in front of the door. The snow is still falling, but again nowhere near as heavy as it was last night.

'Where the hell is he?' Frankie says, whether to himself or the rest of us is unclear. There are no footprints outside, any would have been lost with the continued fall of the snow.

Frankie closes the door and turns to face us. 'Right, everyone get wrapped up and let's get outside, he could of wandered out when he was pissed, check the cars and around the cabin. Don't wander too far, keep the cabin in sight.'

We all recognise when Frankie is serious and there is definitely something wrong. It just seems to be really bizarre as to where the Ranger could be, if he's not in the cabin, he could only be outside which is a really frightening thought.

Without a word, we all head to our rooms and get our outdoor gear on. All our boots are by the front door and we put them on as we head out. The floor is still wet from someone's boots, probably the Rangers as he was last one in.

We all file out of the front door and look around, the silence envelopes house and surrounding area, even the birdsong is muted by the snow this morning. The snow still falls, but only slowly now in large white flakes which are pristine and they cover the ground in a deep blanket. It's like a different snow than what falls in Glasgow which seems to come down dirty and just ends up as a grey slush on the pavements and roads.

The wind that blows through the snow laden boughs of the trees is the only sound that can be heard.

We step down onto the thick blanket of snow outside of the porch and the crunching of the snow under feet interrupts the silence that feels oppressive. We all head off in our different directions, clouds of breath preceding us as we move in different directions.

The large snowflakes spiral their way down from the white fluffy clouds above and start sticking to us as soon as we leave the cover of the porch.

Me and Bobby head towards the cars to check them out and the rest of the lads head around the cabin and into the woods. We move towards the Rangers jeep with some trepidation, Frankie has got us worried as to what we may find, I'm just hoping the silly bloody Ranger hasn't gone and frozen to death.

I move around to the driver's side of the jeep and hold my breath as I slowly wipe the snow off the side window and look into the front seats. With a loud exhale, relief floods through me as thankfully there is no one in there. I look at Bobby and he just grimaces and I can see he is as worried as me. I hurriedly wipe the snow off the back window and I can see there is no one in the back either.

We move to our four wheel drive and an icy fear grips me as I reach up to wipe the snow from the window worried that if he isn't in his own vehicle then surely he can only be in ours. But once again I clear the snow from the windows and there is no one in the front or the back of the vehicle.

'Thank Christ for that.' I say to Bobby with an almost hysterical laugh of release. Bobby's teeth are chattering, I think he may be about to have a break down, he's always been a bit highly strung.

Just as we are turning to make our way towards the woods, we hear shouting coming from the back of the cabin. As we race around the back of the cabin as best we can in the deepening snow, we recognise Davey's voice shouting for us all and there is panic in his voice as he continues to call for us.

We start running again towards the sound of his voice which is further from the cabin than we first thought. Dread grips me as I have a terrible feeling about what is causing the panic that I can hear in Davey's voice.

The snow continues to fall around us as we head into the woods, we see Frankie running ahead of us to where Davey's voice is coming from. The bright white of the snow is contrasted by the dark and gloom under the canopy of the trees and it takes a few moments for our eyes to adjust to the darker surroundings.

Frankie starts to slow and we can see Davey who is standing and looking at something at the foot of a tree, but Frankie is between whatever it is and us. We slow to a walk and catch up with Frankie who has come to a standstill and we move to the side of him.

'Oh, Jesus Christ.' I say, Bobby is dumbstruck and Frankie is just mumbling something incoherently. Razor runs up from the other side of the cabin and comes to a sudden stop as he arrives at the side of us.

What is it boys, what's the big.....' That was as far as he got before he sees the Ranger at the base of the tree. He turned straight around and his breakfast exploded straight out of his mouth. Razor falls to his knees and is still retching as we stand there and try to comprehend what we are seeing at the base of the tree.

Ranger Robert is sitting at the base of the tree frozen white, but this is not the thing that has shocked us all into silence or made Razor puke his breakfast up. It is the fact that our Ranger friend has had his throat cut from ear to ear. The blood that has flowed from the gaping wound across his throat has frozen all the way down the front of his jacket and onto his lap, it has pooled around his legs and in the snow.

The contrast between the pure white of the snow and the crimson of the blood is mesmerising as we continue to stare at it.

What makes the whole situation much more grotesque is that the Ranger's eyes are wide open and they seem to have a look of terror in them.

Razor has recovered but can't face looking at the Ranger again and he just stands there dithering. Whether this is from the cold or the shock or the murder, I'm unsure of but I suspect a little bit of both. The knife which has been used to do this to the Ranger looks like a very large kitchen knife and is lying next to him also covered in his blood. All in all, it is not only a gruesome sight but quite terrifying as well.

Frankie is the first to recover from his reverie. 'How could this have happened?' Even as he said it, you could see the pieces of the puzzle falling into place. We have all seen some horrible things in our lives, but as tough as some of the lads are, this has shaken them to the core.

'Everyone back into the cabin now, there's someone out here and he may not have left.' Frankie says.

It is these spoken words that cause us all to look at one another for the first time and I can see the disbelief in the other's eyes. It's like one of those stupid American horror films where a group of friends are trapped somewhere while a murderer goes about killing everyone.

'Now, yer pricks.' Frankie roars. It's as if we are awoken from a slumber, all this seems to have been happening as if in a dream or underwater. We all turn and sprint as fast as possible around to the front of the cabin and in through the front door.

Frankie slams the door shut behind us and engages the locks, he moves to the window at the side of the door and looks out. He is happy that no one is out front and he turns and heads towards the kitchen. He grabs the nearest bottle and pulls glasses off the shelf, he pours a large measure in each of them and he then drinks his down in one.

We all follow suit and as the warming effect of the whiskey rolls down our throats and courses through our bodies, we all turn to look at Frankie, who looks absolutely shit scared.

## Chapter 14

'Right, everyone go and check all the windows are locked and then get your arses back in here.' Frankie has taken the role of the leader of the group and we all need someone in charge at the moment. We all head to our own rooms initially and then Bobby checks the bathroom and I head back into the living room where everyone has started gathering again.

All the windows are locked and secure and we all feel a little better for this. Being in the room all together gives us a feeling of protection, this is our gang and no one can get in between us. We'll protect each other until the very end. We seem to revel in this calm for a while which gives us time to think about what has happened and what to do next.

'What's going on Frankie?' I ask.

'You know as much as me. We all need to keep calm and focus on keeping safe until we can get the fuck out of here. No one goes outside for anything and we all stay in sight of one another, understand?' We all nod our agreement and to be fair, no one wants to go outside. It's too much to think about the Ranger out in the snow with a wide gaping gap where his throat was.

I get some wood from the side of the wood burner and stock it up and Bobby throws some in the range to make sure we get the room warm enough to try and take the chill out of the air. I'm not sure whether the room is cold or whether it is just that we are internally chilled by what has happened.

'Don't use too much of the wood, we need to make it last. There's some on the porch but the rest is in the wood store at the back of the cabin and I don't want anyone having to go back around there.' Davey speaks for the first time since he found the body of the Ranger. I see Bobby look towards him, a look of suspicion crossing his face. He catches me looking at him and I shake my head for him not to go there.

'What are we going to do?' Razor asks. 'He said we could be here for another few days, maybe even a week, what if whoever has done that comes back?, I'm so scared man.' Razor's voice wavers as he finishes.

'Calm down Razor. That's why we all need to stick together, whoever it is won't be able to get to us if we stick together.' Frankie's voice doesn't match the certainty of his words and there's something about the way he's looking at us one by one that makes me think there is something that he isn't telling us.

'What's going on Frankie, what is it you're not sharing with us?' I ask.

He looks up at me, angry as if I'd said something wrong and his voice shakes as he says. 'I'll tell you what's wrong boys, while you were all checking your windows, I was checking the top drawer over by the sink. The knife that cut that poor boy's throat was one of the set from in that drawer.' He looks around at us one by one again.

'Do you not get it fellas? Either he took the knife out with him and cut his own fucking throat or one of you boys didn't quite take a shine to him.' We all look at Frankie too dumbfounded by his words as they sink in.

Again, whether it's what Frankie is saying or the magnitude of the situation that makes it all feel a little dream like. I have a deep sense of foreboding and still feel as if I'm wading through treacle as I try to gather my thoughts and I think we must all feeling the same.

'Are you on drugs Frankie?' Davey finally says as it dawns on him what Frankie has insinuated. 'What? Suddenly one of us has become a murderer after thirty years of not being a murderer? What have you been smoking boy? And what about you Frankie, do you include yourself as a potential murderer as you're the one who is handy with the kitchen knives after all?' Davey is clearly angry at the implication and his face displays that anger quite clearly.

'I'm not joking Davey, how do you explain the kitchen knife used to kill him being from that drawer? It was there yesterday, I used it at breakfast, and I knew I couldn't find it this morning and *that*,

out there is the reason why.' Frankie's voice is raised while he delivers this last bit of news.
He is clearly upset and actually looks terrified at the prospect of one of us being a killer. If truth be told, he is starting to scare me as well, I feel like I've stepped into the Twilight Zone or something.

'No.' It's Razor who speaks next, 'No. No. No. No Frankie, we're not killers, no one here could have done that, we're all good people here Frankie. We've all been friends for far too long for you to put that on us, look around for God's sake man, come on, point the finger at who you think cut that poor bastards throat in cold blood?' Razor is visibly distressed and he wipes away the tears that have spilled down his face and Frankie has difficulty meeting Razor's eyes.

'Maybe the Ranger heard or saw something or someone outside and took the knife with him for a bit of protection? Maybe he saw someone at the cars or something and felt he needed to confront them, but was attacked instead? There has surely got to be a better and more logical explanation to it than one of us being a murderer?' I ask the questions in a hurry, unsure as to how people will respond, a couple of them nod at my suggestions and

Frankie stares at me as if to say how dare I question what he has said. He looks away and you can almost see him mulling it over in his head, his head lowers as if the weight of what he has said is too much to carry.

There is a hiatus as we all look around, it's quite unbelievable that anyone in this room could have done something so terrible. Some people can't make eye contact with each other at the moment as it is really hard to conceive that anyone has that hatred within them, but most of us have been in situations where we have used violence and sometimes extreme violence when required, so it is not beyond any of us. But murder is surely a whole different ball game, not just scrapping or giving someone a kicking but it's about taking someone's life.

So, is there really a question to be answered, do we really know each other as well as we think, I ask myself? I wouldn't dare say it out loud, it would cause mayhem amongst us. But as I look around the room at each of my friends, the question still lingers.

I look at Frankie, a big brooding and angry man who lost the love of his life so young, leaving him to care for his twins. We know he is still grieving even after all these years and he is still angry over Maggie's death, could that push you over the edge?

Then there's Davey, beaten by his father from a young age and grew to watch him beat his Mum as well. I've seen the man fight, he is an animal and he has that burning hatred that I've seen when he has looked at Bobby this week. But again, could he actually murder a complete stranger in cold blood for no apparent reason, someone he seemingly liked and got along well with?

Razor? This seems the funniest notion, I know drugs can mess you up and he has certainly taken more than his fair share. But is this an example of them making you paranoid and psychotic? I couldn't believe it of Razor as he really is so laid back, he is virtually horizontal and his reaction to finding the Ranger surely said that he was innocent.

And what about Bobby? No, that is just too bizarre to believe, he is just such a soft shite, I don't think he could manage it if he tried. He's on the verge of a nervous breakdown as it is with the stress of the last few days. But aren't you always meant to be wary of the quiet or timid ones. Or is this only in the movies? No, Bobby really is the arse we believe him to be.

So that only leaves me and *I'm* quite sure it wasn't me, I think I would have remembered sneaking out of the cabin in the depths of a storm and cutting some poor sods throat. Yes, I have had a tough upbringing, but I was surrounded by people who loved and cared for me and Marie. Is that what the others will see when they look at me or will they view me with suspicion, someone who could commit murder?

I look up to see Bobby looking at me; it's like he's seen what I'm thinking. He looks towards Davey and then back at me, I shake my head again to say don't even think about it. If something is said now, it could lead to blood being spilt again and I don't think any of us could handle that right now. But I see he has the bit between his teeth and I hold my breath as I see him speak.

'I think you could be right Frankie.' He says in that annoying nasally voice of his, everyone raises their head and turns to look towards him.

'What are you talking about for God's sake?' Razor is still too upset to see what is about to happen, but I can read Bobby like a book and I twitch as he opens his mouth and starts to speak.

'I mean Davey did try to kill me the night before in the woods, maybe he took his frustrations out on that poor Ranger.'

If this was meant to antagonise, he certainly hits the spot. The minute the last syllable leaves his mouth, there is an explosion of bodies as first Davey jumps up followed by Frankie, Razor and me.

Davey is like a bull charging at Bobby and it hardly makes a difference as we all cling on to this raging beast of a man. It is only through Bobby's quick movement that he evades Davey's grasp. Davey is roaring at Bobby like a man possessed about how he's going to 'Kill the weasely bastard'.

Frankie is taking a ride on Davey's back and now has him in a choke hold. Me and Razor are holding tight to his lower half and legs and the three of us are starting to make an impression at last. To be fair, Frankie is stopping his oxygen, so that is probably the biggest factor. Davey slows down and then comes to a stop and drops to his knees making wheezing sounds.

Frankie starts to release the pressure. 'Now you just settle down Davey or I'll have to choke you again. And you, you little bastard, why don't you just fuck off to your room?' He says breathlessly. Bobby is at the other side of the room and is reluctant to move while Davey is still glaring at him the hate clear and blazing in his eyes. Bobby moves across to the kitchen which is as far as he wants to go.

'I thought we had to stay together so no one gets killed, that's what you said Frankie?' Bobby squirms as he says it, I don't think anyone else would give a toss if someone killed the little shit right at this very moment.

'If you're going to stay in this room, you best keep that mouth shut boy.' I say to him. Everyone just looks away from him in disgust. We are all breathing heavy, trying to catch our breath in case it all goes off again.

But this bullshit isn't helping things and Frankie looks at Davey and says 'Are you alright son, you've got to let this go for now, we'll pick it up at a later time. We're all stressed and bloody scared right now and it won't help us if we are all on edge worrying about you trying to brain that little prick.'

Davey rises to his haunches and we all get ready for another round of fun, but he just drops himself down heavily on the sofa and everyone visibly relaxes, well almost. 'To be fair Frankie, if you hadn't come out with such shite in the first place, maybe none of this would have happened.'

For the first time in as long as I can remember, Frankie actually looks a little rattled by what Davey has said to him. Usually his word is law and we are quite happy with things that way, but this challenge from Davey has broken the equilibrium and maybe Frankie should have taken his own advice and 'engaged the brain before engaging the mouth'.

The fear that we are feeling and the paranoia it has caused amongst us is starting to tell. The tension in the room is tangible and is dangerously high amongst the group of people who once considered themselves the closest of friends.

How could this have happened in such a short space of time? I suggest that we all to go off into our own rooms to create a bit of space from one another, just to give ourselves time to calm down and think things through a little. This will allow us to gather our thoughts and think through some of issues that are racing around our heads and maybe allow us to work out the details and ensure that we can remain friends after we get out of here.

We all need some time to clear our heads and think through what has happened and how we move on from here. We have years of friendship which is potentially at risk if we don't all calm down. Then there is the small problem of there being a murderer either inside or outside of the cabin and so we need to stop bickering and make this our priority right now.

## Chapter 15

I lay on the sofa as Bobby has gone to our room and everyone else is in their own rooms and I think about what might have actually happened to the Ranger and why. I discount Frankie's theory of it being one of us. Maybe it was something personal against the Ranger and the person followed him up the mountain when he came to see us, but where would they have waited?

They would have frozen to death out there unless the culprit had a vehicle on the other side of the fallen trees? Maybe they waited until it was late and came up to the cabin and the Ranger has seen them and they struggled, the killer has taken the knife off him and used it to kill him? Maybe they have killed him and moved back down the mountain and driven away or their psychotic tendency has been satisfied and they have left?

I'm trying to think why he would have left the cabin and what he must have seen to think that he needed a knife for protection. He must know this area like the back of his hand, so for him to take a knife he must have seen someone or something outside that he thought was a threat. What about someone else who lives in one of the other cabins, maybe one of them is some sort of crazy?

As my mind continues to wander, the lads start coming back into the living space one by one, obviously having had time to clear their heads and run through differing scenarios as I have done.

Frankie fills the kettle and puts it on the stove and starts to make drinks for everyone.

As far as I see it, we only have a couple of options if I am right and the killer isn't amongst us. One, we sit tight and if the killer is still out there, we can wait them out until the snow thaws or maybe the Ranger Service sends out a rescue party looking for their man.

Or two, we get our gear together and drive as far as we can and then hike the rest. Although the storm isn't as wild as last night, the wind is still blowing and it's still snowing and the snow is deep. I'm not sure we would get very far even in the four wheel drive or by foot.

Davey sits forward and we all sit up. Bobby sits on a stool in the kitchen out of the way, but if Davey went for him, we would struggle to get there. 'What about the Rangers radio, I know it wouldn't work in the storm yesterday, but the weather has settled down a bit, it might work now?'

We all sit further up in our seats at this, he might be right, I remember the Ranger saying something about the radio last night. If we could get to his radio, it could be our chance to get off the mountain without any further damage, physically or mentally. We could radio the Ranger station and get them to send the police, army, the navy or even the stinking RAF if it gets us out of here alive.

'I remember him telling me that he has a radio in the car and a hand held radio which is on the Ranger, the only problem with that is that they are both out there.' Razor says pointing towards one of the windows. 'Who's going to be stupid enough to risk going out there with a crazy on the loose?' The room is quiet as we all contemplate Razor's words.

'I'll go.' Everyone turns to look back at Davey. 'I'll go. If there is anyone out there, I'll tear their fucking heads off and shit down the hole. I'm not having some crack-pot keeping me locked up in here, I'll take something with me, a knife or some other sort of weapon.' I think he is pulling on his cape out of retirement and is going to be the defender of the weak.

'Don't be stupid Davey, we're better off in here together were we can watch out for one another.' Frankie says and looks to us all for support.

'You've changed your tune, the way you were telling it before, we would be better off out of the cabin!' Davey says this in such a way that he is making it clear that something is broken in our friendship, which I'm not sure if we will be able to repair.

'Come on Davey, you know what I'm saying, in or out of the cabin there are risks. But at least in here we have each other's backs and if what I have said is right, we can protect each other in here at least. If what I have said is wrong and I hope to God I am, then we are safe in here. If you go out there, there's no way we can protect you and whoever did this is a fucking maniac.' Frankie pleads with Davey and we all feel a little uncomfortable with the thought of there being a maniac inside or outside of the cabin.

'What about if two of us go out, that way there are always at least two people together at a time.' Bobby pipes up from the kitchen, something we weren't expecting.

'What, you want to go out with Davey do you?' Razor laughs sardonically, I'm not sure if he wants to send out Bobby with Davey just to see him get a kicking after his carry on today.

I suggest that me, Bobby and Razor go out to the jeep and see if we can get the radio working, make contact with the Ranger station and get some help up here as quick as possible. Frankie and Davey can lock the door and watch from the cabin to make sure we are safe. Bobby is the geek, so he will be the best to work out the radio.

There is a brief challenge from Frankie who wants us to stick together as there is safety in numbers. But in the end we all agree to the plan and razor grabs a knife from the kitchen drawer and I pick up a log from beside the fire. This is the best protection we have, but it will have to suffice and I'm really hoping that we won't need it. We get our cold weather gear on and head towards the door ready to move as quickly as possible.

'We'll have your backs from here boys, you can be sure of that, just get us some help.' Frankie tells us as he puts his hand on the door handle and unbolts the final lock and opens the door. 'Good luck.'

I can see he is scared and I feel some trepidation that our 'leader' actually looks terrified. He pulls open the door and we step out onto the porch checking around the immediate area. We head quickly and as stealthily as possible across to the jeep, we look back as we hear the door shut behind us. My stomach is churning as we head towards the jeep which is once more covered in snow so we can't see what's inside.

I look at Razor who nods and with an outstretched arm I wipe the snow from the glass on the driver and rear passenger windows. My heart pounds and feels like it may actually burst out of my chest which is only slightly louder than the rushing of blood in my ears.

I look in both windows and see there is no one in the jeep, but it is dark inside as the rest of the windows are still covered in snow. I tell Razor to clear the rest of the windows on the jeep and I open the driver's door so Bobby can get inside. Me and Razor are the sentries and we scan the area around us for any sign of this lunatic who has filled us all with fear and consternation.

'Shit.' Bobby says and bangs the dashboard which makes me almost jump out of my skin. I lean into the driver's side of the jeep as Razor opens the passenger side door and we both see what Bobby has seen, the radio has been ripped out of its holder and there is now only a jumble of wires where it should have been. I get an uneasy feeling in the pit of my stomach that this nightmare isn't over, in fact it may be just beginning.

'Right,' I say, 'let's get our arses back to the cabin pronto.' We get out of the jeep, slamming the doors behind us and run quickly to the cabin, the door opens as we reach it and Frankie ushers us inside.

'That was a bit too quick boys, what's wrong?' He asks as he closes and relocks the door behind us.

We both catch our breath as we all stand just inside the doorway. 'Whoever did that to the Ranger has trashed the radio as well, there's no help there.' Razor says to Frankie and Davey and then hangs his head. 'I'm scared fellas, I'm not ashamed to say it. Whoever killed the Ranger doesn't want us to get help and it looks like they don't want us to leave either.'

We're all stunned by this bit of insight by Razor as if we hadn't had time to process the information and reach this conclusion ourselves. This trip is turning into a nightmare, everything that could have went wrong has gone wrong and I'm with Razor, I'm feeling terrified at the thought of someone stalking us out there, potentially waiting to do to us what he has done to the Ranger. 'Bollocks' is the only word uttered in the following seconds.

We sit around stunned for a couple more minutes wondering what the hell is going on and why it is happening. What kind of twisted bastard would do that to the poor Ranger and if killing one person wasn't enough, it seems likely that they may potentially want to kill more, if not all of us.

There is a real nervous energy in the room now that is almost tangible and Davey looks like he is about ready to explode and charge out of the cabin looking for the killer.

'What about the radio that the Ranger has, the hand held one.' Razor looks around at us.

'What about it?' Frankie replies. 'Surely you can't be thinking of going back out there after what you've just said?' He is incredulous at the thought that Razor could possibly be thinking of going outside and risking his life.

'What other choice do we have Frankie? If there is a remote chance that the radio is there and that it works, surely we have to risk it? We can just do the same as we have just done and go out as a team and watch each other's back. What does everyone think?' Razor seems to have developed the capacity to think laterally, maybe we have been a bit unfair to him, or maybe he has always just played up to the crowd?

'I think that it's the only plan we have at the moment to get out of here or just bring some help.' Razor puts in before anyone else can speak and he is right of course, our options are limited at the moment.

'We can take weapons with us and watch each other's back, we will just make sure we shout and scream if anything happens. You boys can listen out for us and come running if we need you.' Bobby says. Everyone is surprised that Bobby has volunteered at all and is unsure what to say.

Finally, Frankie says. 'I'd sooner we all just stayed inside and kept the cabin locked up tight.'

'No, let them go, I can't stay cooped up in here and if they get the radio, at least we can get some help here quicker.' Davey says. Frankie and me look at Davey, we're probably thinking the same thing, he probably wants Bobby to get his throat cut.

'Yeah, cheers for that vote of confidence Davey!' Razor says. Davey just stares at him blankly and I'm unsure what Davey's motive is for sending us out there.

Weapons of choice are limited, me and Razor stick with what we have and I see Bobby pick up another knife out of the drawer.

We are all armed and ready to go out again, we are all feeling uneasy about this as the Ranger is within the woods and out of sight of the cabin.

There is only one back window in one of the bedrooms and that doesn't have line of sight to the Ranger. The wood store is at the rear of the cabin and the other bedrooms have windows on the side of the cabin.

We zip our coats up again and put our hats and gloves back on and make our way towards the door. 'Wait' Frankie says and we can all see he is actually really worried for us. 'Don't go out there boys, I'm not sure it's the right thing to do.'

'It's alright Frankie,' Razor says, 'we'll be fine, we've got each other's backs. You boys just watch out for each other.' The way Razor says it, it is unclear if he means look after each other or really watch your own backs. We unbolt the door and slowly head out into the snow, our heads moving from side to side looking for any sign of movement or danger.

The fresh snow crunches under our feet as we make our way around to the back of the cabin. If I let my imagination run away with me, it sounds as though we are squelching across a sea of bones and bloody bodies.

I try to rein my imagination in at this point as it's not helping one iota right at this moment. We make our way between the pines and across to where the Ranger is still lying at the base of the tree. We are wary and as we keep an eye out for danger, our heads are bobbing up and down like I've seen a pack of meerkats do at the zoo. It appears safe and there seems to be no one around, so we move towards the Ranger.

'Oh man,' Razor says, 'this is fucking gross, I don't think I can go near him!'

'It's ok Razor, I'll take a look.' I say and hand him the log that I have taken as protection. I move across to the Ranger and take my gloves off so that I can unzip the front of his coat, I immediately feel the cold start to sting my fingers.

It's really disgusting even though the blood is frozen and as I crouch down and start to unzip the Rangers jacket, all I can think is please let the radio be there. It's the last thing I remember as I feel something solid hit me on the back of the head and everything goes black.

I don't know how long I've been lying there, but as I start to regain consciousness, I struggle to see as my vision is blurred. What is making it harder is the brightness of the snow in front of my eyes which causes me momentary blindness; it is so white, pristine and pure and as I start to raise myself off the floor, I see drops of red falling into the whiteness.

My head swims and It's difficult to focus, I can't seem to think what the red could be that is interrupting the pureness of the snow.

'Jack, Jack, are you okay man? Are you okay, stay there and don't move.' I raise my head to see where the voices are coming from and I see two shapes coming at me quickly. I jerk backwards trying to create space between myself and whoever is running at me, but as I do, a wave of nausea hits me and I fall back to the ground and lay looking up at the canopy of trees above me. I'm not sure if I'm dying, but I seem to have no strength at all left in me and everything goes black again.

## Chapter 16

'Jack, Jack yer prick, wake up will you. It's okay Jack, you're safe. It's me Frankie and Davey's here too. We need to get you back to the cabin. Do you know what happened, where is Razor?' There's an urgency to Frankie's questions and I can start to make their faces out and I see them casting anxious glances around them, but there are just too many questions that I can't seem to focus on them.

I let Frankie and Davey lift me and part carry, part drag me back to the front of the cabin and inside.

Davey throws me onto the sofa and Frankie goes and locks up the front door. Everything is still a blur and I see Davey looking at me with a mix of emotions, part worried, part angry and part something else that I can't quite understand. I'm still confused as to what has happened and how I came to be on the floor outside the cabin.

Frankie goes to the kitchen and gets some hot water from the kettle and a clean towel out of the drawer. He comes across to where I am lying and tells me to lie still while he takes a look at my head.

'What is it Frankie, what's wrong with my head?' I'm still struggling to focus properly and am wondering how I managed to get the Rangers blood on my hands if it was frozen. And then I feel the pain in my head and I flinch away from Frankie.

'Hold still boy, I can't clean you up if you're going to be acting like a big baby.' Frankie speaks softly to me, something has changed and I can't seem to think straight to understand what it is. My head is really starting to throb now and Frankie describes the cut on my head to me which he says is about five inches long and is pretty open to the elements.

I start to recall the red drops on the snow as I struggled to raise myself and realise that it was my blood falling out of the wound, as is the blood on my hands which wasn't the Rangers after all.

I sit there, my head throbbing and tender as Frankie probes at it to make sure the damage isn't too serious. The ache is tremendous and I'm feeling queasy as he pushes around the edges of the wound.

Frankie tells me the cut probably needs stitches, but he's left his needle and thread at home. This attempt at humour misses its mark for all of us and he hands me the part blood covered towel and tells me to wipe my face and hands clean.

'You'll live son.' Frankie says as he steps back from me. He goes to the kitchen cupboard and he brings back a couple of paracetamol and a bottle of water which he hands to me. I gratefully accept them and put the tablets in my mouth and wash them down with the water. I hope they are fast acting as the pounding in my head is excruciating.

I continue wiping the blood from my hands and face but as I can't see what I'm doing, it's all just guesswork really.

Davey is sat at the kitchen table as Frankie sits down in the chair opposite me. 'Can you tell us what happened Jack? When you hadn't come back after twenty minutes, we knew something was wrong and decided to come looking for you.'

I let the words sink in, but it is difficult to remember details when you're head feels like there is a jackhammer pounding at it. 'I don't really remember too much, I just remember Razor couldn't look at the Ranger or go near him to get the radio and I said I would do it. I crouched down in front of the Ranger and was opening his jacket up to get the radio, when it just all went black.' I pause to take a sip of water that I'm still holding. 'That's about it really, I don't remember anything else. The next thing is you two shaking me awake. Where is everyone, Razor and......?'

I see Frankie look at Davey who is seething as he glares at me. 'We don't know.' Frankie says. 'There's no sign out there, there are tracks into the woods, but we just wanted to get you back in here and find out what happened.' We all lower our heads and look down inwardly contemplating what has happened. My emotions are all over the place and I assume that goes for the others as well.

As the awkward silence continues and no one seems to want to broach the subject, I speak up. 'Does this mean what I think it means?' I ask.

'I guess it does.' Davey replies and I can see him fighting with his emotions as he says 'I just can't believe Razor could have done something like this. Could the drugs have really messed him up so much, it just seems so stupid, unreal?' The last part he says almost to himself as he shakes his head in disbelief trying to make sense of it all.

You can see the conflicting emotions in Davey's face and that he is struggling to believe it himself. Out of all of us, Davey and Razor were the closest. I think Davey always felt like Razor's protector because Razor was 'harmless' and would never 'hurt a fly'. How stupid does that sound now and I think this is the cause of the conflict for Davey that I saw earlier.

'I just can't understand why he left you alive Jack, after what he did to the Ranger, why didn't he do the same to you?' Frankie asks the question we have all probably started to think, although I'm just thinking thank God he did.

'I really don't know Frankie, I'm just glad that he didn't kill me, maybe our friendship stopped him, I don't really know. His head must be so messed up though. I'm struggling to really believe that he could have done it at all.' Davey looks sharply at me as I say this and I think I see a softening in his eyes and a slump of the shoulders as if he appreciates that somebody else understands his torment.

I'm wondering what part Bobby played in saving me or stopping Razor, but Frankie or Davey don't even mention Bobby which has me thinking the worse. What have they seen outside, is Bobby dead or has Razor taken him somewhere? Or are they in this together?

We sit around in silence for what seems an age before I speak up. 'What are we going to do now?' Frankie and Davey both look at me, I can see the conflicting emotions of anger and fear cross their faces.

'I don't know, I really don't know.' Frankie says, his head hung low, the burden of the latest events weighing heavily on his mind. 'We should just sit tight until the storm passes and we can get out of here.' He finally says.

'I want to go out and find that prick and kill him.' Davey speaks in a monotone, his face is blank now as if he has resigned himself to what has happened. There is just a quiet and ominous anger bubbling just below the surface and I fear for Razor when Davey gets his hands on him, I think he could really kill him.

'That's enough talking about killing Davey.' Frankie says. 'I've had about enough death to last me a lifetime and longer, let's just sit tight and wait it out. We've got enough food and drink to last us; it would be stupid to go out there. No, let's just sit and wait. Surely he will get hungry or thirsty and possibly even die of hypothermia and save us all the trouble of ringing his bloody neck.' I think that maybe this will just make him more desperate and we don't know what that will make him do.

We sit and digest what Frankie has said and although it makes sense, I feel uneasy sitting in the room with these two giants who could turn on me at any moment. I can't even believe I am thinking this about these guys who are my best friends, but the events of the last twenty four hours have made me us all more than a little paranoid.

'I know you won't like this, but I'm with Davey and I think we should go out and try and find Razor, I think we're like sitting ducks in here?' I cautiously say trying not to provoke Frankie into a reaction. I look at Davey right in the eye; he shows no emotion but gives an imperceptible nod in my direction.

I need an ally in this and if he wants to go out, then I'm more than happy to go with him and 'hunt' down Razor. I have no intention of trying to kill him, but at least we're not sitting around waiting for him to come for us, it would at least give us a fighting chance.

'No,' Frankie raises his voice, his face starts to redden. 'We stick together, look what happened when we decided to leave the cabin last time, we stay here and wait this out, I'm not losing anyone else. I've got to get back. I've got to get back to the twins!'

We both stare at Frankie, his eyes moist with tears, this is the first time I have seen Frankie like this since he lost Maggie. I think the thought of not seeing the twins or the twins possibly losing both their parents is all too much for him. They are his world and he has been so protective over them over the years, he is genuinely scared he may not see them again. He turns away from our stares, embarrassed by his show of emotion.

'Okay, okay.' I say, I'm not comfortable with doing nothing, but seeing Frankie like this really brings it home and can't help thinking about getting back to my own kids. Davey just lowers his head, I can tell he doesn't want this, but will go along with it.

He breathes deeply in and out, whether this is to calm his nerves or the fact that he is a ball of pent up rage is my overriding image of Davey. I think he is probably trying his best to will himself to stay calm and not fly out of the door after Razor.

I get up and grab a bottle of scotch and three glasses and head back to the sitting area. I pour three generous measures and push them towards the others. 'Cheers.' I say sardonically. No one replies, they just nurse their drinks taking small sips. After the first round, Frankie pours another three drinks and this carries on until the bottle is empty.

Minutes turn to hours as we sit in virtual silence, waiting for something to happen. It remains deathly quiet inside and outside of the cabin except for the crackling of the logs in the wood burner.

Occasionally we talk about Razor and what could have driven him to do this, Davey and Frankie talk about the neglect Razor and the kids suffered growing up and maybe the weed being a way to manage that anger or whatever it is. I carefully raise the issue of the time that I saw him buying heroin, Frankie and

Davey stare at me and are incredulous as to why I didn't raise it with them before. I try to explain the position I felt I was in, wanting to let them know, but feeling a sense of betrayal to Razor if I did. They both look at me as I say this and there is and understanding if not acceptance in their faces as to my reasoning. I also say that I did keep an eye out for him and tried to 'monitor' him for any change in behaviour to do with addiction.

I told them that I even spent hours on the internet looking up signs of heroin addiction to make sure I knew the symptoms that I should be looking for.

Eventually we start to discuss how we are going to manage the next couple of days and agree that someone should always be awake during the day or night and that we will regularly check that the cabin is locked down securely.

There is a small pile of logs left next to the wood burner and there is still a small pile out on the front porch, but not enough to keep the wood burner alight for a couple of days. We decide to cross that bridge when we get down to the last few logs of wood.

We discuss when we should leave, there is only a light fall of snow now, but there must be several feet of snow on the ground. In certain parts, it has drifted against trees and is even deeper, but we think the four wheel drive should be able to get through it once it starts to thaw. We think about the car and hope that it starts and runs ok, but we decide not to worry about that at this time, as we don't need it just yet.

It's late now and we are all feeling tired and the whisky hasn't helped, Frankie says he will take first watch and me and Davey head towards our rooms. Just before we head in, Davey turns to Frankie, 'You stay awake now big man, no sleeping on the job.'

'Aye.' Is all Frankie says as we head into our rooms and close the doors behind us. I consider putting something up against the door in case there is an enemy within, but decide against it as Frankie won't be able to get in and wake me up when it is my watch.

I think it will be hard to get to sleep considering what has happened today and the level of mistrust and paranoia surrounding the three of us remaining in the cabin. I stay fully clothed but take my boots off as I climb onto the bed and pull the blankets over me. As my head hits the pillow, I feel a weariness creep over me and it isn't long before I am fast asleep.

A nagging doubt enters my mind as to what happened when Razor struck me on the head and what part Bobby has had to play in all of the day's events and where are they now?

I dream of crimson on white and a darkness where something feral lurks waiting to kill. Images of sharp teeth and steely eyes waiting to devour flesh on the mountainside leaves me sweating as I sleep.

## Chapter 17

I am away to the world in a deep sleep and my head swims when I feel someone shaking me and I hear Frankie's voice calling to me after what feels like only five minutes As I drag myself from the bed he tells me I've been asleep for over four hours.

We decided that each watch would be four hours, which would mean that after the first four hour stint, everyone would get eight hours sleep. This would hopefully ensure we all had enough rest and we would be alert in case anything happened. I grab my boots from my room and head out to the living area.

I'm still groggy as Frankie heads to his room, but as only Frankie can, there is a full pot of coffee made which should help pick me up and keep me awake for as long as needed. I head to the sink and turn on the cold tap and splash some cold water on my face,

I almost splash it over my hair but remember the cut on my head at the last second. The cold water both shocks and invigorates me and I grab a towel from the drawer and dry myself as I look out of the window across the white wilderness. I look at the peace, tranquillity and beauty right outside of the kitchen window and think how it looks so perfect, but I know that it really hides a multitude of sins.

As I turn away from the window, a shooting pain drives through my skull where my head injury is, this makes me gasp with the pain and so I grab a couple of pain killers and head over to the coffee. I pour a mug, pull out a chair and sit down at the dining table knowing that if I sit on the sofa I could doze off. I swallow the pain killers and pick up a boxing magazine that Davey has brought along and start my watch.

The first hour passes slowly and without incident and I am starting to feel tired so I get up to put the kettle on to boil and I head towards the windows to take a look out. There is a white blanket of snow covering the ground and nothing stirs as I look out onto the white crispness that covers the ground plants and trees. It looks absolutely beautiful, so picturesque almost like a Christmas card.

It is quite light out there as the moon is up and there doesn't seem to be any cloud cover obscuring its reflected light which illuminates the whiteness of the snow. I can see quite well out of the windows and there is no one in sight and I head back to the toilet to take a leak, all that coffee has kept me awake, but also bloated me. I go back to the kitchen and sit at the table and start a game of patience with the cards.

I don't know how long I have sat there playing as I'm lost in my reverie before I hear the noise that breaks the silence. I'm not sure what the noise is, I just know something has broken the silence that has enveloped the cabin over the last few hours.

And then I smell it, smoke. I turn sharply towards the sleeping quarters, but there are no obvious signs of fire, but I now hear the noise again and it is the crackling of something burning and I can smell the smoke even more strongly now and this triggers me into action, I run towards the bedrooms and bang on the doors, shouting to Davey and Frankie.

I now see smoke curling under the door to my room and before I have time to think about it, I throw the door open. This was a mistake, the fire sucks in the oxygen from the cabin and blows me back from the door. My shirt sleeve has caught fire and I feel rough hands grabbing at me. It is Frankie, he drags me away from the flames and pats my arm between his hands to put the flame out.

The door to my bedroom is between the living area and Davey's room, we see Davey on the other side of the flames, that are raging now and Davey can't get past. Frankie shouts to him to shut his door and break his window to get out and come around the front.

Frankie and I run to the living area where he grabs two of the fire extinguishers there, instead of handing one to me, he tells me to go and let Davey in and then heads to the back of the cabin where the fire is raging. I head to the front door and unbolt it, I am expecting Davey to be there about now, but when I open the door, he is nowhere in sight. I shout out calling his name, but there is no response. I look back towards where Frankie is, but he is too busy trying to dampen the flames down.

I'm struck by indecision, should I stay and help Frankie or should I go to see where Davey is, he could be in trouble, he could have hurt himself or maybe something worse. I make the decision to go and find Davey. I grab my boots that I placed next to the front door, fasten them quickly, and then grab my coat off the hook.

I look back at Frankie one more time but he hasn't taken his eyes off the fire and so I head out into the snow. I zip the front of my jacket as I go up and turn towards the back of the cabin, I shout out to Davey in what can only be described as a loud whisper. It is deadly silent out here now, the fire is only a quiet crackling as I come around the side of the building to where Davey's room is, I see that his window is smashed and there is broken glass all around the floor, but there is no sign of Davey.

'Davey.' I whisper, 'Where the fuck are you man.' I turn away from the cabin and that is when I see two figures in the tree line, one is on his knees and the other seems to be holding him by the throat. Because it is dark under the trees, it is difficult to make out who it is.

I shout out to Davey and as I do, the figure who is standing turns to face me and then turns away and runs into the woods. I move cautiously towards the kneeling figure and feel a sense of dread crawling up my spine, as I get closer, my worst fears are realised and I see Davey on his hands and knees in the snow.

I run the last few metres to him, but I can already see the blood that surrounds him on the ground and I stop dead in my tracks. With a great effort, Davey pushes himself back on to his knees. As I move next to him, I can see a large piece of glass that I assume is from the window lodged in his throat. I kneel down next to him and I can see the blood oozing out of the wound, pulsing with his heartbeat. I put my hand to it, not to pull it free, but just to see if I can stop the blood pumping from the wound.

As I do, I look into Davey's eyes and for the first time ever, I see fear in Davey's eyes, he reaches out and grabs my hand and I think it is to stop me pulling the glass free. 'It's okay Davey, don't move, I'm just trying to stop the bleeding.'

He reaches then and grabs the collar of my coat and he starts to pull me down to him and his face turns from fear to anger, but the strain is making the blood pulse out of the wound even faster, I can feel its heat oozing faster between my fingers and I realise nothing is going to stem the flow. The muscles in his neck stand out and are like tense cords and as he opens his mouth to speak, blood flows out from between his lips.

'What is it Davey, who did this, was it Razor, where is he, was Bobby with him?' Davey looks at me and I can see the futility enter his eyes at last, but he manages to utter one word before his strength leaves him and I see the lights go out behind his eyes. Davey falls forward into me and I hold onto him hoping that he may just survive.

I hold onto him for what seems a long time, but can only be minutes. I eventually drop to my knees and I gently lower him to the ground and look into his still open eyes, I run my hands over his lids like I've seen them do in the films and his eyes close.

This is surreal and I'm struggling to believe what has happened, Davey is dead, the man mountain was just a man after all and Razor or Bobby have done it, how could they have done this to one of our best friends? I actually feel an ache where my heart is thinking about the big man being dead, a chasm has opened up and I feel like I might fall through it. Crimson on white, the image will stay with me forever.

Thinking of Razor or Bobby doing this to Davey stirs me from my reverie and I realise that I'm out here with a maniac, I need to get back to the cabin and warn Frankie. I stand up and look around deep into the trees. There seems to be no one about but it is dark under the boughs of the pine and a shiver runs down my spine to think of them out there possibly watching me.

Tears are streaming from my eyes and I slowly start to move towards cabin. I continue to look all around me as I make my way to the front of the cabin, all my senses on alert for any noise or sight of our 'friends' Razor or Bobby, whichever one of them is the murderer.

My mind is a blur and my emotions are in shreds as I try to comprehend what is happening. How could have someone we have known all our lives and trusted to the point of making them Godfathers to our kids have done this to his best friend.

Tears continue to roll down my cheeks and although my head aches, my heart seems to be in a lot more pain at the moment. I think of the Ranger dying alone up on the mountain away from his family and friends. I think of wee Mary and the boys and how they will cope knowing their big man isn't coming home and I think of Donna, Tony and Rosie if it does or doesn't turn out to be Razor doing these terrible things.

And then I think of Bobby, the loner, the one who needed us more than we needed him. He leaves no one, no family. His only friends are here with him...........dying on the side of a mountain.

I'm finding it all too much as I step onto the porch and see that the front door is ajar and this sends a jolt of fear along my spine. I can't remember if I closed it behind me when I went to look for Davey and I slowly push it open further. I wipe my eyes as my vision is blurred with tears and I notice that my hands and coat are covered with blood, Davey's blood. This almost makes me stumble and retch.

I take a couple of deep breaths to calm myself and step across the threshold and see that there is no one in the living area or kitchen that I can see and so I close and bolt the door behind me. I move slowly into the kitchen, trying to keep as much of the cabin in my eye line and I open the set of drawers where I reach in and take one of the sharp knives out.

I look around the cabin once more, checking the door and windows are all secure and I move to the living room.

The acrid smell of smoke still hangs in the air although the fire seems to be out as there is no sound of burning timber just the cracking and movement of ancient timber. I give a low shout out to Frankie but there is no response, I'm worried that whoever was out there has managed to get in whilst I wasn't here and get to Frankie. If they killed Davey, they could kill Frankie with ease, particularly if he has been distracted by the fire.

I continue to move slowly through the cabin towards the bedrooms and the scene of the fire. There are small sounds from ahead, are these just the timbers cracking and moving as a result of the fire or is it the sound of someone in the cabin, I can't tell at the moment.

The fear and adrenaline I'm feeling is causing my senses to overreact and I am terrified of being attacked and killed like Davey and the Ranger. I can still see the blood vividly as it streamed down the front of their jackets as their lives bled away from them. I am edgy and shaking as I try to keep the fear at bay long enough to find Frankie so we can get out of this situation alive, I think the two of us together stand a greater chance of survival. My heart pounds in my chest as I struggle to control my emotions.

I reach what was my room and look into the charred remains, everything is blackened. It is soaking wet with water from the extinguishers, three of them lay on their sides just inside the door. Frankie isn't in there, but I also need to be wary of this room as the window is completely smashed where Razor or Bobby have broken it and started the fire. I move on to what was Razor's room and the door is open here, I edge around the frame cautiously and look inside, but the room is empty.

Frankie's room is next, but the door is shut and I'm not sure I have the courage to continue forward. I take a couple of deep breaths trying to steady myself and it works to a degree as I hadn't even realised that I was holding my breath. I reach out and grab the handle and lower it cautiously, I decide at the last second to throw the door open as quickly as possible hoping to surprise anyone if they are in there.

To my relief Frankie's room is also empty and the bathroom is opposite with its door wide open and I see that it is also empty.

This only leaves Davey's room and this door is also closed. I go through the same preparation as I did for Frankie's room and I grab the handle and throw the door open. There is no one in there and the curtains blow in the wind where Davey had smashed the window right out when escaping the burning cabin.

I relax slightly and look behind me to check the coast is clear as I move slowly across the threshold and into Davey's room. As I look around his room, there are reminders of the big man everywhere, his clothes, trainers, after shave and there beside the bed on a small set of drawers is a picture.

I lift the picture frame off the drawers and look at the image, it is Davey with the boys, one in each arm and Mary standing in front of them dwarfed by the size of Davey. I suddenly sob at this image of my friend and his family and how happy they seem and wish that we could all go back in time to when that photo was taken.

I am unexpectedly grabbed by someone through the window and I scream out, I am terrified at the thought that someone is about to kill me.

'Shut up yer fool, it's me, keep the fucking noise down.' Frankie leans in and I see him for the first time and I am not reassured. 'Stand Back, I'm coming back through the window as you've locked me out the front.' Frankie clambers through the window, his big frame moving with ease as if he does this sort of thing all the time.

'Where the hell have you been I whisper to him?' Some of my composure returns, but not all of it.
'I've been outside looking for you, when I eventually got the fire out, there was no sign of you or Davey and the door was wide open, I didn't know what had happened.' It's at this point I see his eyes are drawn to the blood that has covered the front of my coat and is all over my hands.

'It's Davey's blood, I found him at the edge of the woods, I saw whoever it was with him, but I couldn't make out who it was. I don't know what happened, I couldn't save him, he was on his knees...............I was just too late to do anything.' Once again a sob escapes my throat and I hang my head in shame, not quite sure what for, possibly for choosing now to fall apart or not being able to save my friends. My devastation as to what is happening with my friends threatens to swamp me and drag me down into despair.

'I just don't know what to do, I'm so scared we're not going to get out of this.' My body shakes with grief and I feel myself falling apart.

Frankie moves across to me and in a rare show of affection puts his arms around me. 'Don't blame yourself Jack, you wouldn't be the one we expected to save anyone. It should have been me or Davey saving you and it looks like we have both failed now.' He steps back and looks at me and I look up. 'But let's not beat around the bush though son, we know who did this and he needs to pay for it. But as I see it, we've only really got one option left to us now.'

## Chapter 18

'What option have we got, Frankie, this fucking lunatic is going to kill us all.' In my heart, I don't believe that we will get off the mountain alive. The pressure in my head has been building since the Ranger was killed and I feel like a dam is about to burst, crack by crack.

'Pull yourself together Jack, it's no use falling apart now son. We've got to keep it together, we've got to stick together, we'll get through this if we are there for each other. We *will* survive this Jack, we will.' This last part is a statement, Frankie really believes it, it's why we have always considered him the leader of the group, he is so headstrong and has great belief in his own ability to succeed.

'I'm sorry Frankie, but this is all just too much. I don't have your confidence, I don't have your determination or your strength, how will *I* survive this?' I don't moan or whine as I say this, it is a genuine question, I fear for my life after what has happened over the last couple of days, my face is damp with tears as I fail miserably to control my emotions.

'I know son, but you need to stay strong now, we're stronger together, we can cover each other and we can watch each other's backs. We can get through this if we just stick together, strength doesn't matter, look what happened to……….Davey.' His voice fails him as he says this, but picks up again. 'Come on boy, stay strong, let's do this together, we can make it home.'

It's like a motivational team speech that some guru could give to some wanker office workers who are into that sort of thing, talking about profit margins and strategies.

But when it is a matter of life and death, it takes on a whole different meaning and the hollowness of the words eats into me. I lift my head and nod to him as if it has made a difference, but I'm not really sure that any words could reassure me at this point.

Frankie tells me to get my rucksack and pack some food, water, matches and some spare warm weather clothes out of the other rooms. I don't think he thought that one through, my room is burnt out, Davey was six foot four and nearly as broad and Razor was all skin and bone. Bobby's kit was in our room, so I'll get no joy there.

He goes to pack himself while I look for something suitable, I have to drag myself around to do this, I feel as if I am slipping into a deep depression and am struggling to motivate myself. It's like wading through treacle or being neck deep in water and trying to run, you just can't seem to do it and my progress is slow.

Frankie is packed first and calls me into the kitchen. I think he can see how upset I am and how difficult this has become for me and he starts to put some biscuits, bread and a tin of corned beef into my rucksack. He adds a couple of bottles of water, the rucksacks can't be too heavy, and he wants us to be able to move quickly when we go. He looks up and takes a deep breath and exhales before he says, 'Come on Jack, we've got to keep it together, we've all been through some tough times and this is the toughest, but we'll get through it and we we'll get home together.'

He describes the plan to me and it makes some sense, he tells me that we are going to take it in stages, but we are going to try and plan for every eventuality. He says that if we try and stay in the cabin we will be sitting ducks and Razor could start another fire and force us into the open.

At least by being on the move and getting a bit of a head start, we might just be able to get through this. So we wrap ourselves up, jackets fastened, hat and gloves on, rucksacks on our backs and four by four keys in hand.

The first stage of the journey will be to try and drive the four by four as far as the fallen trees and then march quick time down to the next cabin. If the couple are there that the Ranger mentioned, we will try and see if they have any way of contacting the outside world and if not, hopefully they will have a vehicle that we can get away in.

If worst comes to worst, it's the next cabin on the way down and we will use each cabin as a stepping stone going down the mountain until we get to the bottom and then we will wing it from there. We're hoping someone may have a hunting rifle or similar in one of the cabins that we could use to protect ourselves. Although this seems very unlikely, it is something to aim for and something that gives us just a glimmer of hope.

'Are we ready to go then Jack?' Frankie looks carefully at me as he says this. He's looking for confirmation that I am not going to fall apart again and probably be of some use to him on the journey.

'I'm ready Frankie, let's go home.' I say this with more certainty than I'm actually feeling but there is no point in dwelling on this, if I'm going to die I want to go down fighting. Frankie nods and I think he is feeling the same way, we aren't going to stay here and be an easy target for Razor if it is him doing this, but I still have my doubts.

'Right, remember to keep moving whatever happens. Get into the car, any problems, we slip right back out onto the road and get going. Let's go.' He is our or should I say my leader once more.

We unlock the door and pull it open and Frankie looks around the tree line and moves steadily out of the cabin onto the porch, I follow him again feeling like some sort of hunted animal, understanding that I am the prey in the relationship. It is slightly lighter than it has been as the morning approaches and visibility is slightly improved.

We move quickly down to the four by four our boots crunching the snow beneath us and wipe snow from the side windows and look inside, all is clear. Frankie unlocks the car and climbs in the driver's seat and I get into the passenger seat. It is a bit cumbersome with our rucksacks on, but we don't want to take them off just in case. Frankie ratchets the seat back a little to make easier for him to drive.

Frankie puts the key into the ignition, depresses the clutch and turns the key. Nothing. He turns it to off and tries again with the same result. I can feel the pressure in my head building as I realise that this part of the journey has ended before it's begun.

'Shit.' He says and then looks at the dashboard, where there isn't even a light on. 'Someone's fucked around with the electrics or disconnected the battery or something, do you want to take a look or shall we stick to the plan and move on?'

'Let's just stick to the plan, I don't want to have to start messing under the bonnet and be exposed out there. Anyway, if it's the electrics that have been cut or something, there'll be nothing we can do about it and we will be too vulnerable out there.' I say this with certainty knowing any change in the plan could put us in more danger.

''You're right son, let's just stick to the plan and keep moving and get to the next cabin.' Frankie scans the surrounding area once more and opens his door, I follow suit and we both move quickly along the track that leads to the road. The plan is to stick to the road all the way to the next cabin, this way we will hopefully be able to see anyone coming at us from any direction.

The snow is actually deeper on the road which means it will make the journey a little harder and a little slower for us, but we think this is the best approach. The other option is to walk under the shelter of the pines, but it is dark under the canopy of the trees and visibility isn't as good which could hinder our progress or allow someone to get close without being seen.

We are moving along the track that leads to the road and making steady pace even though the snow is a real encumbrance. We reach the road that leads down the mountain and pause to look around and make sure that we are not being followed and that there is no one in the surrounding woods, our fear makes us hypersensitive to every sound or movement.

It is cold and our boots and trousers are soaked, I'm starting to think that this might be more difficult than we first thought, but it is only about a mile and I'm sure we can make it. The snow is even deeper on the road than on the track if that is possible and we move to the centre of it and start the trek down.

The going is slow as we wade through the knee deep snow, it is tiring to as we have to raise our feet high to be able to step properly. We both stumble a number of times as our legs begin to grow weary, but at least we are heading down the incline. We don't talk too much as we use all our energy to walk whilst trying to listen out for noise around us as we constantly observe the tree line and the gloomy woods that surround us.

The main words passed between us are usually expletives when we trip or stumble and fall forwards into the crisp snow. The cold bites at my legs as it is reaching above my knees and soaking through my trousers but I just keep stepping forward. Our breathing and the crunching of our boots in the snow is now the only sound in my ears.

As I look at the snow, I think back to growing up and playing in the streets where I grew up. If we had snow like this when I was a kid, it would have been wonderful, building snowmen, snowball fights and sledding down the road. I can't remember the snow ever being this crisp or clean, it was usually dirty by the time it reached the ground and it just got worse as it picked up the grime and dirt from the floor.

You would always have to be careful making a snowman or throwing snowballs as you were just as likely to pick up a piece of dog shit as the snow. We used to call these type of snowballs 'dirty bombs' and this was before any of us had ever heard of chemical warfare.

'Jack……….Jack'

I'm broken out of my reverie by the sound of Frankie calling my name, I'm not sure how long I've been daydreaming, but we have reached the fallen trees in the road. It's a good job Frankie has stayed alert, we could have been murdered in the middle of the road if it was down to me to be vigilant. I think it is the continuous glare from the snow and the repetition of putting one step in front of the other that makes you start to lose concentration and drift off.

The snow is unbroken all around us until it reaches the trees and it is clean and unblemished, there has certainly been no one travelling up this stretch of road before us.

There are two giant pines across the road, one lying flat and one caught in the branches of the tree opposite. The snow has piled up against the trees and it has formed a formidable barrier, there is no way that we would have got the four by four past this point even if it was working.

'Let's take a couple of minutes to get our breath and give our legs a rest before we crack on.' Frankie says. Even he is starting to feel the pace and I'm hoping that the other cabin isn't too much further on. The early morning gloom is starting to lift and there is a brightening of daylight as we sit on a branch of the fallen tree, we are both breathing heavy as we sit there and there isn't any small talk.

We take a couple of gulps of water from our water bottles when suddenly, a number of birds burst from their hiding places and fly straight up and away above our heads. This startles us both and we both jump to our feet at once and look in the direction of where the birds took flight from. We don't see anything, but something must have scared them to leave their branches or nests.

'What do you think? I ask Frankie in a hushed voice, 'Do you think it is him?' I turn to look at Frankie, but he doesn't take his eyes off the woods.

'I don't know Jack, it could have been anything, but we don't want to be taking any chances. Let's get moving.' We are not fully recovered, but Frankie is right, we need to keep moving and get to the next cabin. I keep my concentration this time, my head turning from side to side and my eyes darting in all directions.

We both keep looking behind us and I'm not sure if it is my imagination, but I swear I keep seeing shapes behind the trees. Because of the distance and the poor light in the woods, I don't want to say anything to Frankie as at the moment I can't be certain. It may just be the nerves and paranoia that has enveloped us all these last couple of days and I'm seeing shadows were there may not be any.

We keep walking as fast as we are able to in the deep snow, our breath clouding in front of our face showing the strain that this march is putting on our legs and our lungs. But we can't stop, we can't let Razor or Bobby catch us in the open like this, we have to get to that cabin and have some respite from this exhausting walk.

We are going for another five minutes along the road and just ahead we see the signpost for the cabin, it has a single word painted on it, 'Douglas'. I remember the name now, the Ranger mentioned Mr and Mrs Douglas were the owners of the cabin and he didn't manage to reach them before the storm took hold. So maybe, just maybe they will still be here and we can get away from this nightmare.

We take a last look around to make sure were not being followed and then head along the track that leads to the Douglas's cabin. It is only about twenty metres back from the road and it is a small cabin, probably only half the size of the one we have been staying in.

Right away we can see that there is no vehicle in front of the cabin and we know we are out of luck in that respect. We head up to the porch and try the front door, but it is locked and Frankie looks through the tall window to the side of it.

I turn and cast my eye across the woods and that's when I see him, I can't make out any features, but I see him just behind a tree in the shade of the woods.

'Shit Frankie, he's out there.' I almost shriek at him and he turns quickly to look in the direction I am looking, but as quickly as I saw him, he has gone again and I can't see him anymore, it's like he's just blended back into the woods.

'Where Jack, where is he?' Frankie's frustration at not being able to see who I saw is evident as he stares intensely into the gloom of the woods.

'He's gone, but I swear Frankie, I swear I saw him standing just behind a tree a few metres back into the woods, but it's like he just melted back into the trees again.' I strain my eyes to see if I can make anything out, but I can't see him any longer.

'Right, we need to get into this cabin and see what they've got for weapons, I know it's extremely unlikely, but maybe they do a bit of hunting or something while they're up here.' Frankie puts his boot through the window at the side of the door, it is a tall window about eighteen inches wide and the same height as the door.

He uses his elbow and his gloved hand to break away the sharp shards that surround the hole. It isn't wide enough for us to get through with our packs on and so we take them off, throw them through the window and climb through sideways after them.

'Give me a hand with this.' Frankie calls to me as he takes one end of a pine kitchen table. 'We'll stand it up against the gap and it will give us a bit of warning if the bastard tries to follow us in. You start checking the cupboards and drawers for any weapons and I'll go and make sure all the windows are secure and there are no other access points in here.'

I start opening all the cupboards and pulling out drawers looking for something that may be used to save our lives. There doesn't seem to be anything of use and I start to feel the futility of the search. I can see that there is nothing of use in the final drawer and I throw the drawer across the room in frustration. Frankie comes rushing out of one of the back rooms thinking something is happening.

'It's okay, there's just nothing that we can use as a weapon. Even the knives that they've got are crap, you've got more chance of getting a paper cut.' My little tantrum is over and so I start closing the cupboard doors and pushing the drawers back into place, I go and retrieve the one I've flung across the room gathering in papers that it contained.

I push it back into place and turn to look at the rest of the room, this is an old couple's cottage and I don't suppose they were expecting to have to defend themselves against a raving lunatic.

This makes me laugh out loud and Frankie looks at me as if I am losing the plot.

'It's okay.' I say again, 'I was just thinking of a raving lunatic and I thought of Razor and his dancing from his 'rave' days.' Frankie gets the joke and a sad smile crosses his lips. He goes to the sink and takes two glasses from the shelf above and draws off two glasses of water and hands one to me.

We both drink greedily and we fill them again but take our time with the second ones, we both stand with our backs to the wall, catching our breath and staring at the door and the table in front of the broken window.

And we wait.

## Chapter 19

After we have caught our breath and calmed down somewhat, we begin to discuss the next stage of the journey. We know we have to be wary of Razor or Bobby, but we also have to keep moving. We can't just stay in the cabin as we would be as much sitting ducks in here as we were in the other cabin.

It would only take a fire to make us abandon the cabin and leave us exposed to whatever Razor or Bobby had planned. It would be better if we left in our own time with a plan as opposed to running from a fire in blind panic.

We think that the next cabin down is closer to us than this one was to our cabin and that we might be able to reach it quicker. We decide to take in some nourishment while we wait and we open our packs and take a couple of apples and a packet of chocolate biscuits out that we have brought with us from our supplies and eat while we can.

We are tired from the effects of little sleep and the slog through the snow and it is important that we eat and drink while we can, not knowing when we will eat again. All the time, we keep a watch on the front door and the window where we broke in waiting for someone to come through it. Our nerves are becoming frayed and it won't be long before someone cracks and yes, that someone will probably be me.

'I still can't believe what's happened, it really is like a bad dream.' I say to myself as much as I say to Frankie. 'This is crazy, just plain crazy. This is the most difficult time in my life regardless of what's happened in the past.'

'Yeah,' Frankie says quietly, 'It's certainly right up there. I never thought that we would lose each other this way, I always thought that we would be friends until the day………………' Frankie stops, realising what he was about to say. We both drop our heads knowing that 'the day we die' was meant to be a long way away and we were expected to die of old age not at the hands of a killer on the side of a mountain. And that the killer would be one of our own.

'Right.' Frankie says after a few more seconds of silence. 'Getting morose isn't going to help us get off this mountain, we need to stay positive and focussed so let's get our stuff together and get moving. We don't want to get stuck out in bad weather or the dark.'

We pack the remainder of the biscuits away and fasten our packs back up, zip our coats up and put on our hat and gloves. We are ready to go again and I look at Frankie and he nods to the door. We make our way over to the door and Frankie peers around the edge of the table to make sure the coast is clear and no one is waiting outside the window.

He gives the all clear to remove the table and we both grab a side and move it out of the way. Once again, Frankie slowly leans out of the window peering from side to side to make sure we can get out of the cabin safely without being attacked.

'I'll go first and you pass the packs out to me and then you come out. That way I can make sure we don't get any nasty surprises.' Frankie leaves his pack in front of the door and carefully steps out onto the porch and I see him turn and check the surrounding tree line. 'Pass out the packs Jack, quickly now.' I pass Frankie's pack out first and then my own and clamber through the gap after them. Frankie is just finishing putting his on and fastens it and then he helps me putting mine on.

'Right, let's get going son before we change our mind, back onto the road and then as quickly as we can down to the next cabin.' We step off the porch and move onto the track, the snow is not as heavy on the track as it has some shelter from the branches of the pines. It is still hard going as the muscle in my legs remembers the strenuous repetition of walking through the deep snow.

We are about halfway along the track when I catch movement out of the corner of my eye and I turn to see a figure running towards us through the trees, I see the glint of a knife in one of his hands and my heart leaps as the fear takes hold. I almost yelp and then I scream to Frankie, 'RUN Frankie, run.' I head off into the treeline heading away from our pursuer down the incline of the mountain and Frankie realises there is danger and starts to sprint after me.

'Jack……..Jack, what is it?' He shouts after me as we weave between the trees and the undergrowth, the snow is sparse here due to the overhanging branches of the pine trees and we can move much quicker although the trees have now become a danger because of the low hanging branches that whip and scratch across our faces.

'Just fucking run Frankie, he's got a knife.' I shout back to him in a breathless voice. We run for what seems a long time and I feel my lungs are about to burst and I stumble and fall flat to the ground, kicking up dirt and pine needles into my face. I feel a strong hand grab my shoulder and I scream out thinking I'm about to die.

'Ssshhhhh.' Frankie hisses at me and I realise that it is him that is trying to turn me over. I turn and manage to get into a sitting position, sucking in great gulps of air, even though it is freezing, I feel perspiration forming on my face and neck. We have come to a stop in a small clearing where the soil has given way to rock.

Frankie is on one knee and facing the way that we have come from, his eyes scan the trees but it is so dark under the trees as light fails to make it all the way through the canopy above. The only sounds we can hear is our laboured breathing as we sit here waiting, watching and listening. No one seems to be out there and Frankie's posture softens as he senses no immediate danger, he takes a deep breath and turns towards me.

'What the fuck happened Jack, I couldn't see a thing behind me as I was running, what did you see?' Frankie is looking at me like I'm a fucking moron or something which really pisses me off.

'Fuck Frankie, I've just saved our arses there, spotting him coming through the trees with a big fucking knife, don't look at me like I'm fucking stupid, Jesus Christ!' I am so annoyed by Frankie's display of superiority, I could throttle him myself.

'Alright, alright Jack, just calm yourself down. I just meant I looked back a couple of times when we started running and I didn't see anyone, I'm not saying you didn't, but there are lots of shadows in the trees and maybe you thought you saw something?'

'Seriously Frankie, you think I'm making this up, you think I'm seeing things now. I know what I saw, I saw him running through the trees and I saw he had a knife in his hand and he would have got us too if I hadn't seen him first.' My ire is rising and Frankie can see this and holds up his hands in a placating gesture.

'Okay Jack, I believe you, but we're both tired and stressed, so let's not be losing it out here in the open.' Frankie turns back away from me and scans through the trees again to make sure no one is out there. It's then that it happens, I don't know where he comes from, but I am shoved out of the way and strike my head on the floor and everything is a haze as I see the blade arcing down towards Frankie.

Frankie senses the movement behind him and turns towards his attacker just as the knife drives down, it catches him straight across the face and I see a spray of blood erupt from the deep wound. Frankie falls backward as his assailant jumps on to him and raises the knife again to bury into Frankie. I feel drunk and am unable to move to help him and I feel at a loss as to why I have suddenly lost the use of my limbs. I am only seeing things through a fog and seem to have lost all control of my body.

As I look, something else catches my eye in the woods and I see another figure charging through the trees screaming like a banshee and I see that it is…………Razor and I can't comprehend what is happening, I thought Razor was dead.

Razor comes charging right at me and hits me across the face with a log, my head fly's backwards, followed by my body and all I can see are stars. I land on my back and can feel the shape of the water bottles in my pack pressing into the base of my spine. I still don't understand what is happening and as my vision starts to clear, I feel the warmth of blood running freely across my forehead, into my ears and down the back of my neck.

I stare up at the canopy above, the bright sky and I cough. I can hear words being spoken, maybe shouted or screamed. I can't make them out and I'm not sure who is shouting them. I can't seem to move my head or lift it to see what has happened, who had attacked Frankie and where the *fuck* had Razor come from. And why do I think Razor is dead?

As my head clears, I see Razor come into view and stand above me, he is still holding the log that he hit me with and I try to speak but only a croak escapes my throat. My mouth is dry and I try to swallow. 'Razor………what happened?' I see Razor looking down at me, he looks so pale and I see him holding his stomach, there is blood soaking through his jacket and also down his trousers.

'I'll tell you what happened you fucking murdering bastard.' I see a tear escape the corner of one of Razor's eyes as he speaks with such malice to me that I don't really understand what he is talking about. 'You killed the Ranger, you tried to kill me, you killed Davey and you've just tried to kill Frankie you fuck.'

My head spins, what is he talking about, how could I have tried to kill anyone? 'But Razor, I've been attacked too. Me and Frankie thought it was you who killed the Ranger and Davey and where is Bobby, we thought you'd killed him too?

'Who the fuck is Bobby you idiot, you kept talking about him as you attacked me and stuck a knife into me, you are a fuckin' lunatic man and you won't be murdering anyone else yer wee prick.' As he says this, Razor raises the log above his head and

I hear Bobby laughing and I hear Davey say 'YOU' before he died in my arms. It is then that brings the log down on my head again and again until I am dead.

## Chapter 20

'Frankie, are you okay mate. It's Razor, are you ok?' Frankie slowly opens his eyes and sees a dishevelled and white as a sheet Razor above him. He grabs the collars of his coat and tries to pull him down, but he doesn't have the strength.

'Stop fussin' big man, it's alright, you are safe now, Razor to the rescue. We've got to get back to the other cabin, you've got one bad ass cut across your face and we need to get it covered up or it might be affecting your chances with the ladies.' Razor laughs at his own wit and starts to pull Frankie up off the ground with a grunt.

'What happened Razor? I thought it was you that was killing us all off.' As Frankie says this, he starts to remember being attacked and that it wasn't by Razor, but by Jack and this confuses him as he can't seem to gather his thoughts enough to think it through.

The agonising pain in face is also distracting him and as he tries to touch it, Razor grabs his hand and says that he doesn't want to do that or he will have a world of pain. Razor explains that he has an opening down the side of his face from his temple to his chin and it is about as wide as the Grand Canyon.

'You were a lucky boy Frankie, how he never cut your throat is a mystery and it was a good job I arrived when I did or you'd be as dead as the others now. I think we have a story to tell our kids and grandkids now, they probably won't believe it, but we will have the scars to prove it.

Razor pulls Frankie to his feet and they stumble through the trees, but eventually make it back to the Douglas's cabin where they climb in through the broken window. Razor sits Frankie down on one of the kitchen chairs and pulls the table back across in front of him, he then heads to the kettle and fills it with water and puts it on the stove.

The Douglas' cabin has a standard gas cooker with gas canisters stored outside, thankfully, they haven't turned them off and they light first time. He lights the oven and the gas fire as well to get some heat into the room. While he does this, he roots through the cupboard and finds a couple of mugs, coffee, painkillers, a large bowl and some clean cloths.

Razor rips down some curtains from one of the bedrooms and finds a pack of drawing pins in one of the drawers, he proceeds to pin the curtains across the broken window to keep some of the heat in the room. He then grabs the first aid box off the wall next to the kitchen cupboards and puts it on the table, Frankie opens it to see what is inside that they can use.

By the time Razor's finished, the water in the kettle is starting to boil and he goes back to the stove and makes two cups of black coffee and pours some of the water into the bowl and then puts them all on the table. Frankie has sat and watched him do all this in amazement, Razor has seemed to be enjoying himself, taking charge and getting organised.

But even though Frankie is finding it hard to focus due to the pain in his face, he also notices that Razor is struggling and he winces now and again as he moves around the cabin. The blood on his top and down the front of his trousers is substantial and Frankie is worried about how badly Razor is hurt

Razor passes Frankie a coffee and tells him to be careful as it's hot and then dips a cloth into the water and wrings it out. He sits on a chair next to Frankie and starts to gently wash Frankie's face clean of the blood that is covering it.

When he's done this and rinses the blood out, he says, 'Right Frankie, now this is gonna bloody hurt.' Even more carefully, Razor starts to clean around the wound, it causes Frankie to wince and take a sharp intake of breath but he holds himself steady.

'What happened Razor, what the hell has happened the last couple of days? What made Jack do these things, he was so normal as we made our way down the mountain, he was upset at the loss of the Ranger and Davey and how it was you of all people who had killed them. He was a fucking nuisance and I know he was always the butt of the jokes, but to murder or try to murder his friends, what's that all about?'

Razor smiles sadly at the unnecessary deaths of his friends and the Ranger, a man they had all come to like after a night of drinking and sharing stories. 'It's quite sad really Frankie, sad that we didn't recognise what was happening to Jack, what was going on in his head. You're right, he was a pain in the arse and we did take the piss out of him unmercifully, but he was still one of us, he was always there at the most important times as we grew up.

He was at our weddings, wetting the babies heads, when we brawled, when we lost our loved ones and somehow, we, his only friends didn't recognise just how fucked up he was…………………and it could have been all our fault.' Razor says this with finality, as if he has come to terms with the role he has played in what has happened.

Razor finishes cleaning off Frankie's face and takes a large dressing out of the first aid kit and gently places it over the wound on Frankie's face. He asks Frankie to hold the dressing where it is while he uses the medical tape to secure it in place.

'What do you mean son, our fault, what did we do to drive him to murder?' Frankie seems to know and to understand what has happened but he still needs the confirmation from Razor.

'We pushed too far and too hard Frankie, you had to have been there to really see how much he'd lost it. I don't know the medical or psychiatric terms for it, whether it's split personality, schizophrenia or something else, but Jack wasn't one person anymore, he had become two people and the other one was called Bobby.' Razor looks tired and takes a seat at the table and takes a sip of his coffee.

'When we went to get the radio from the Ranger, Jack could barely look at him, the blood was thick down the front of the Rangers jacket and the gaping wound at his throat was horrible. So I handed him my knife whilst I crouched down to unzip the Rangers jacket. I unzipped his jacket and reached in and took out the radio, it was clean as the Rangers waterproof coat had helped keep the blood from soaking through. I stood up and turned around and I knew then something was wrong, but I just couldn't work out what it was. I know now that it was Jack, he was looking down at the Ranger, right at his cut throat after telling me he couldn't bear to look.

So I say to him 'What the fuck Jack, I thought you couldn't look?' And then he lifts his head and he smiles at me and I think he's laughing at me for making me get the radio through the blood and gore. But he steps towards me and before I know it he has stuck the knife right into my stomach, I didn't realise it was the knife at first, I thought he had punched me and all the time he has this stupid smile on his face and as I try to step away because he is freaking me out now, my leg gives way under me.

I fall to one knee and I look down thinking I've tripped on something and that is when I see the handle of the knife sticking out of me.

I try to speak, but as I do, the shock seems to have knocked the wind out of me and I'm thinking to myself that this is absolutely fucking weird and I look at Jack and he is still smiling and he says to me. 'A wee shite am I Razor, a gobshite, a prick, the butt of everyone's jokes since we were kids, well who's laughing now'.

And I finally say out loud, 'But Jack.' He cuts me off and says Jack isn't here, it's Bobby who you've name called like a bunch of kids all your lives and he is talking in this whiny voice like it's a caricature of his own voice and I can't seem to focus to understand what he means, I'm just thinking who the fuck is Bobby?

I'm starting to feel light headed and I've got my hand at the entry point of the knife and I can feel the blood running through my fingers and I think that this is it, I'm going to die. I fall onto my side and I'm just looking at Jack's boots now and then the voice changes and it's Jack's voice again and he's starts having a conversation with himself and I'm all over the place because I think I'm dying, so I just close my eyes and listen.

'What have you done Bobby, what have you done? It's Razor, he was our friend.' Jack really seems scared at this point as if he has just stumbled across me and 'Bobby'.

'He was *your* friend Jack, not mine, always calling me, slapping me across the head, thinking he was the big man when he was just a pot head.'
'No, no, no Bobby, he was alright Razor, he was funny, he made us all laugh. He's got Donna and Tony and Rosie, who's going to look after them now?'

'I don't care, he was a bastard to me and I'm sick of it, I'm sick of all of them.'

'Let's go and get Frankie and Davey, they can help, they will help keep him alive.' Jack is pleading to himself now.

'No, Razors going into the woods where the others can't find him, look at him anyway, he's already dead.' Jack kicks me at this point and I stay still, hoping they will just leave me there. I'm starting to feel cold now and I sense that I'm losing a lot of blood and then he grabs hold of me by the ankles and start dragging me away.

As he pulls me along, Jack continues this bizarre conversation with himself as if it is two different people, changing speaking styles as he becomes Bobby and then back to Jack again.

It's so sad Frankie, he talks back and forward, 'Bobby' bringing up all the things over the years that we have done to him or called him or left him out of, like being a Godparent, he says he so much wanted to be a Godparent and it was only Jack who let him be one to one of his kids.

And I'm thinking Jack hasn't got kids, he's not even married, he's lived in that apartment in the city centre on his own playing with his computers all day earning a fortune.

Jack then tells Bobby that Frankie saved him from the bullies at school when the boys set his shoes on fire and I just want to open my eyes and say no Jack that was you Frankie saved, not 'Bobby'. But I don't, I lay still and let him drag me along. He's finding it hard work and he is breathing heavy, so he drops my legs and leans down to me and before I know it, he pulls out the knife.

I'm expecting a lot of pain, but I'm starting to feel numb and I don't cry out or flinch from the pain and I think this saves my life, although I didn't know that at the time.

Jack asks how this all started, why did he kill the Ranger in the first place, what did the poor Ranger do to deserve what happened? Bobby describes how everyone had gone to bed except for the Ranger and Jack was drunk and then Bobby started talking to him and the Ranger.

The Ranger was drunk and thought it was funny to mock us just like the rest of them and he didn't even know us. Jack or 'Bobby' was in the kitchen and picked up a knife from the drawer and ran from the cabin as if he was upset and the Ranger followed him, trying to coax him inside putting a consoling arm around him and that was when 'Bobby' or Jack or whoever cut his throat.

'Bobby' says he has never laughed so much as the Ranger clutched at his throat and the blood pumped through his fingers, he watched with glee as the Ranger fell back into a sitting position against the tree and the life just left his body.'

Razor pauses at this point to take a breath and gather his thoughts, he is sweating now, and Frankie can see it along his hair line and on his cheeks.

'Are you ok son?' Frankie asks and starts to worry how badly Razor is hurt.

'Aye, I'll be okay, I just need to change this dressing.' Razor gets up unsteadily and takes the bowl and cloth to the sink, empties it out, rinses it clean and fills it again from the kettle. He returns to the table with the bowl and a clean cloth and sits back down with a groan.

He turns the first aid kit around to face him and selects a square dressing from it and opens the packet, placing it ready for use on the table. He then slowly takes off his top grimacing with the effort and Frankie sees the dressing that he has on is blood soaked and is seeping down below the waist of his trousers.

'Shit Razor, how bad is it, are you going to be okay?' There is real concern in Frankie's voice as he realises that Razor is in a lot worse condition than he thought.

'How the fuck do I know Frankie, I'm not a bleedin' doctor.' Razor laughs and grimaces at the same time as he says this and slowly pulls off the tape holding the dressing in place. He lifts the dressing away from the wound and Frankie sees for the first time the extent of the damage the knife has done.

It doesn't actually look too bad at first sight, it is a small gash just over an inch wide, but as Razor grabs the cloth from the hot water, blood is still oozing from the wound and Frankie wonders how much blood Razor has lost since he was stabbed.

Razor cleans the area around the wound and again grimaces in pain as he wipes the cloth across the entry point of the wound. He picks up a dry cloth and dabs it around his stomach to dry it off and then quickly applies the dressing to it. Frankie pulls a few lengths of the medical tape off for him and Razor places them across the dressing and onto his stomach in a criss-cross pattern.

Frankie gets off his chair and moves to Razor and helps him to his feet as he says, 'Come on pal, let's lie you down on the sofa and let you rest. I'm feeling much better now, I can get anything you need.' Razor's pallor is pale and he has a sheen of sweat across his face and brow and Frankie knows that Razor really needs a hospital. Frankie goes back to the table and brings over Razor's coffee and then fetches a chair and his own coffee.

'Are you sure you're okay Razor, shall I get my kit on and try and find help further down the mountain?'
'No Frankie, I'll be okay if I can rest a while and just let you know what happened.' Frankie stands and gets a fresh cloth and runs it under the cold tab and returns to sit next to Razor and wipes the perspiration from Razor's face.

'Look at you Frankie, just like Florence Nightingale.' Razor laughs the thought of Frankie in a nurse's uniform, he thinks he may becoming delirious.

'So, as I'm lying there pretending to be dead, Jack continues the conversation with himself for another couple of minutes as to why 'Bobby' should stop what he is doing and the argument flows backwards and forwards. In the end, Jack says to himself that he needs to get back and is worried how he is going to explain what happened to you and Davey.

That is when Bobby speaks for the last time and chillingly says for Jack not to worry as the pair of you would both be dead soon anyway.

I hear Jack's footsteps recede and I open my eyes almost expecting to see someone called Bobby standing in front of me. He isn't there of course and I have to remind myself that there is no such person. I don't know how he managed to convince you of what happened, but I assume that he blamed me?'

Frankie thinks back to when he and Davey were waiting in the cabin and the minutes ticking by before they eventually made the decision to go out and find Razor and Jack. 'Yes he did. He had that deep cut on his head from where he told us you had clobbered him with his log of wood that he had handed to you.

We believed him obviously, because he was lying there bleeding in the snow. It seems funny now but he must have hit himself really hard to cause the damage that he caused, me and Davey were both convinced. We talked about you and he was so convincing, telling us that he found it so hard to believe that you could have done these things.' Frankie sits forward leaning on his knees with his head hung and Razor thinks he may be feeling a little shame for giving up on his friend so easy.

'So what happened to Davey, how did Jack manage to kill him? Davey was so strong, almost unbeatable.' There is a hint of incredulity but also loss in Razor's voice as he says this. It really is hard to believe that Jack could have bested Davey.

'I don't know, he must have caught him by surprise. He had set a fire in his room while we were asleep and he was supposedly watching out for you. It had us all panicking and Davey had to break out of his window to escape. I sent Jack to open the front door to let Davey come back in. I can only assume Davey has thought that he could catch you if you were close by after setting the fire.

You know that he was our super hero, Davey, man of steel. Somehow, Jack must have lulled Davey into a false sense of security and attacked him, he certainly wouldn't have taken him face on. When I managed to put the fire out, the cabin was empty and so I went back into Jack's room and climbed out the window to see if I could find anyone outside.' Frankie stops as he suddenly remembers something important.

'Shit, I don't believe I missed it. All the broken glass from the window was on the outside of the building, I remember it cracking loudly as I jumped from the window onto the ground.' Frankie shakes his head admonishing himself for what he sees as a glaring oversight.

'What are you talking about Frankie?' Razor asks, not recognising the significance of what Frankie has said.

'The glass is on the outside of the building, you were meant to have broken the window from outside and set fire to the room somehow and because we were in a panic over the fire, I never even thought about the glass. If you had broken the window from the outside, the glass would have been inside the bedroom.

In fact I never even wondered where you would have got matches from to light the fire, they were all in the kitchen by the stove and burner. It all seems so obvious now I think about it, but he was so clever at misdirecting us. Think about the radio in the car and going so far as braining himself to prove you had knocked him out.'

'Don't feel too bad about it Frankie, none of us were smart enough or observant enough to see the changes in Jack, if you think back, there were a lot of clues that we missed even before the trip. In fact, thinking about it now, I can even remember him mentioning a Bobby to me and then quickly telling me that it was one of his cyber buddies or something.'

'I don't know Razor, if I'd been a bit smarter, Davey might still be here with us.' Frankie is still beating himself up over not knowing that it was Jack all along who had committed the atrocities over the last forty eight hours. He is quiet for a moment as it sinks in but eventually asks, 'Anyway Razor, how the hell are you here now, how did you survive?'

## Chapter 20

'Well Frankie, you know how I always tell you what a real man I am, that I'm strong as an ox under this skinny exterior, well I'm about to prove it to you.' Razor smirks and winks at Frankie, showing that he still has that sense of humour that can lift your spirits even in the darkest times like right now.

> 'So, I'm lying there in the snow thinking this is it, I'm about to die but not wanting to obviously. But I pack some snow in front of the wound trying to freeze it or something. I'm not sure why really, but I remember that if you cut something off, like a finger or toe you should pack it in ice to try and save it. That's how my mind was working at that point anyway. And I lie there for another hour or so and I'm freezing and thinking maybe I'm not dying but in a little bit of shock and that maybe the cold has shut off some of my blood circulation. But I'm so tired at this point and before I know it, I've drifted off to sleep.
>
> I'm not sure how long I've been there when I wake up but it is dark and I feel frozen stiff. I hear noises nearby and I think it is Jack come back to check on me, but after a minute, I realise that it's just animals rooting around. And then I start to wonder if there are any bears or wolves on Scottish mountains and if they can smell

blood? I start to move my hands and feet to get some circulation in them and then I manage to prop myself up and get onto my knees and it's then that I start to feel the pain in my stomach and I remember that I have been stabbed. I stand up and have to fight the nausea back down and the light-headedness that I am feeling, I lean against a tree while I get myself together. I'm freezing cold and numb in places but I manage to keep focussed on what I need to do.

After a minute or so of false starts, I start walking in the direction I think the cabin is. This is going to be a slow process as every jarring step sends a shooting pain to my stomach. I can feel blood trickling down my stomach and down my leg and if I don't get some help soon, I know I'll be dead. I have to stop regularly to catch my breath as the exertion of putting one foot in front of the other takes a tremendous effort.

I reach the Ranger and I have to take a break and I lower myself against a tree. Even though it is freezing, sweat is running down my face, my neck and my back with the effort that it is taking to get to the cabin. My throat is dry and I'm struggling to swallow and I pick up some snow from the ground and put a small amount in my mouth. The sharpness of the ice crystals gives me brain freeze and I squint my eyes together until it passes and I manage to swallow some of the snow that is melting in my mouth. This feels good and so I eat a little more over the next couple of minutes.

I notice that the sky is starting to lighten and I'm hoping that I can get to you before Jack can do anything else. I try to stand but my body doesn't respond, whether this is the loss of blood or that the knife wound has done some damage internally, but I just can't get up. I try shouting but my voice is no more than a whisper and this makes me so angry with myself that I start to cry. I feel a big soft shite because I am useless to you and I'm scared that I won't get to you on time.

I manage to stand again with some effort and start my slow walk. I pass the Ranger who is still propped up against the base of the tree and I stumble and fall again. As I try to pull myself together and wipe my tears with the back of my hand, I notice something further along and closer to the cabin, just on the edge of the woods. My stomach turns thinking it might be you or Davey, but I'm really hoping that it is Jack. Whatever happened, I seem to find the determination to move myself and I get onto my hands and knees and start walking on all fours towards the shape on the ground. It takes me about fifteen minutes to go about thirty metres because I have to stop every couple of metres because of the pain and the nausea.

I eventually reach the shape on the ground and I see right away that it is Davey, no one is as big as him and I crawl around to the front of him. He is white with frost and he's got a huge piece of glass sticking out of his throat and blood surrounds his head like a halo. Seeing Davey like this breaks my heart. You know we are tight Frankie, but I think me and Davey were just a little closer. You know how he adored Tony and Rosie when they were little and he was a big help for me when things were really tough. You all were and I couldn't have made it without your help, but seeing Davey like this just broke me and I lay down next to him and just wanted to die there and then. I thought I was too late and that I would get to the cabin and find you dead as well Frankie, I've never felt so sad as I did then, the sorrow was overwhelming.

I'm thinking of Mary and the boys and your twins and all I care about is who the fuck is gonna look after them if I don't get off this mountain. I feel the tears stinging my eyes and running across my face as I lay next to Davey and when I open my eyes again, it is lighter again and the new day seems to give me a new resolve. And it is then that I think to myself that I don't want to die here and I don't want all of those kiddies growing up with no father figure in their lives after what they have all been through. And in my head I'm telling myself to get my lazy arse up and get down the mountain, and that's when I hear the slamming of car doors. And I hear two doors slam, not one and this energises me and I get up on to my knees and stand up slowly because the pain is excruciating.

I start to slowly stagger towards the cabin but it is taking too long and by the time I make it around to the front of the cabin, there is no one in sight. Two car doors stand open and I know that you are still alive and I can see where you have gone, your tracks are heading towards the road. I can't follow you just yet, I need the first aid kit and some painkillers and to try and get warm for a short while before I move on again. I know you will be heading down the mountain and if it was me I'd head for the next cabin down and see what help there was there.

I go into the cabin and take a quick look around to make sure you are either not dead in one of the rooms or that Jack isn't there either. I see where the fire has been in Jack's room and the broken windows. I then go to the burner and throw some of the logs in and get it blazing. I get the pain killers from the cupboard and throw a handful down, I need all the pain relief I can get at the moment. I get the first aid kit, some clean water and a handful of tea towels from the cupboard and start to patch myself up in front of the burner, that wasn't pleasant I can tell you. I manage to patch myself up as best I can and grab some water and chocolate biscuits from the cupboard and try to get something down me before I pass out. After about thirty minutes, I'm feeling about as good as I'm going to feel, I've rehydrated, eaten something but most importantly, the pain relief is working and I feel warm again. I'm feeling weary again and before I know it, I've dozed off.

I wake up with a start and I think that I have been asleep for about an hour. The burner has died down but it is still warm in the cabin but I know

I've got to move or I might never get up again. I have to literally drag myself off the couch and I head to my room to grab my pack to put some supplies in it and change my clothes as they are all blood soaked and wet. I go to the kitchen and grab some water, biscuits, pain killers and the first aid kit, this is about the most I can carry in my condition anyway. I put my cold weather gear back on and head out of the cabin to catch up with you.

Although I see your tracks heading out to the road, I know it will be quicker under the canopy of the trees where the snow isn't as deep and I start my slow walk to chase you down. I know you've got a good lead on me, but the going will be heavier on the road and I don't think you will be moving much quicker than me. I trudge along almost within sight of the road but I don't see any sign of you and I'm getting worried that I've made a mistake, so I move towards the road and I can still see your tracks down the centre of it.

I take a rest against a tree and swallow a couple of more pain killers with some of the water I drink and eat a couple of biscuits too. It's a real struggle to get back up and I feel so nauseous again as my head spins and I need to hold onto the nearest tree. When my head has stopped spinning, I stand up straight and start walking again, following the line of the road as I go. I pass the fallen trees and I keep going until I nearly walk into the cabin, my head is so fuzzy now, I can hardly think straight. I stay at the edge of the woods and when I look, I can see that the window at the side of the door is smashed and I see something leaning against the window and I know that you are in there.

I think of shouting to you, but then I think that this might put you in danger, so I sat down at the base of a tree in the shadows and I waited. I must have dozed off again but wake up to the sound of voices as you are both coming out of the cabin but I couldn't get up off the floor and I watched as you started to head along the track. I was just thinking get up Razor yer tosser, don't let Jack beat you and I found the strength to get myself up going through my routine of nausea and light-headedness.

I move slowly through the trees and I don't know how, but it was like Jack sensed me and he turned and looked right at me and then he just turns and runs shouting for you to follow. I saw you turn and look, but you were looking in the completely wrong direction and then you took off after Jack.

I just thought 'shit', how am I going to catch up with you, but I started a sort of fast walk/stumble to try and catch you. It's a good job Jack is so out of shape from too many burgers and sitting on his arse playing on his computer or I would never have caught you.
As I approach the clearing, I saw you looking in my direction. And then I saw Jack with the knife raised above his head and you turned towards him as if you knew something was wrong but you somehow managed to deflect the knife. There was a spray of blood in the air and I thought I was too late and that he had killed you and I just thought GOD NO. I just started running as fast as I could, picking a branch up off the floor on the run.

I could see him as he climbed on top of you and I started screaming like I was fucking William Wallace and Jack looks up and he is smiling, but when he sees me a look of puzzlement crosses his face and I can see he is thinking how the fuck did I get here and then I hit him as hard as I could with the wood.

And the rest they say is history.

So you see Frankie, I'm a warrior, a real man in Shaggy's body and your saviour, so when the kids ask, you remember to tell them I'm your fucking hero.'

Razor drinks the last of his coffee and hands his mug to Frankie. 'Right, that's all from me, I just need to have a wee nap now to recover some of my super powers. Wake me in about three days please my good man.' And with that, Razor closes his eyes.

Frankie looks at Razor and smiles, Razor has that effect on you, always looking to cheer you up in the darkest times. But Frankie sees the perspiration around Razor's hairline and his unhealthy pallor and he knows that he is in a bad way.

Frankie gets to his feet and starts to gather his kit together, he needs to get off the mountain and get some help for Razor. He knows that if there is no one in any of the other cabins, he will have to make it to the foot of the mountain where there is a farm that they passed when they first turned off onto the mountain Road.

He puts water and some biscuits and a sandwich on the floor next to Razor within easy reach of him, after taking a couple of painkillers himself, he leaves the rest for Razor. He then gets his rucksack and puts a bottle of water and a little food in for himself in case he can't make it down the trail. Frankie gets his cold weather kit back on and looks back to Razor.

'You hang in there Razor, you are my hero and I'm not going to let you die on this Godforsaken mountain.' With that, Frankie carefully pulls on his hat and gloves and heads out to find help.

## Chapter 21 – Four Weeks Later

Frankie and Razor stand at the graveside with their families surrounding them, Mary and the boys stand in the middle of their friends who surround them in a protective huddle. The day is dry and the sun is shining, but an ice cold wind blows that keeps everyone wrapped up and huddled together to ward off the chill. It is still hard to believe that Davey is dead or some of the things we have learned since we survived our trip up the mountain.

♦ ♦ ♦ ♦ ♦ ♦

Fortunately for me, Frankie managed to reach help before it was too late. He had started his trek down the mountain struggling through the snow and the tree line. He passed the next two cabins on the way down, but there was no one in either and Frankie was thinking that he would have to make it all the way down before reaching help.

But just as he had given up hope of getting help before he reached the bottom of the mountain, he heard the rumblings of an engine heading up the mountain road. He ran from the cover of the trees almost being mown down by a mountain rescue jeep that was coming up the hill.

The guys in the jeep see the condition of Frankie and jump out to help him, but he just tells them to get back in and climbs in the back of the jeep and tells them to get up to the Douglas's cabin where he has left me.

The mountain rescue team were actually on the way up to see what had happened to the Ranger. Frankie briefly describes the events of the last few days and tells the rescue team that we will need Police, paramedics and someone to collect the bodies of our friends and the Ranger. The rescue team are shocked by Frankie's revelations, but he tells them to keep driving and concentrate on saving the ones that are alive.

By the time they get to me, I am in a really bad way, I have lost a lot of blood and got some sort of infection which was really starting to kick in. I really don't remember too much about it all as I was out for most of it, but the rescue team call in of all things an RAF helicopter. And where else would it be sent from, but Lossiemouth! As I always said, I love the RAF, they're always there when you need them.

Through some excellent work between the ground crew and the helicopter crew, they winch me and Frankie aboard and fly us to the nearest hospital able to cope with the type of injury and infection that I have which is at Inverness.

I'm in in the hospital for three days and while I am there, Frankie drives home to see the twins, Donna, Tony and Rosie, he also goes to see Mary and the boys. The Police have already broken the news to them and they are obviously devastated by the loss of their big man, but they hug and cling on to Frankie for a while when he is there.

The boys go in the garden to kick a ball about and Frankie tells Mary everything that happened and that there was nothing that we could have done for Davey. Frankie tells Mary that we will all be around at some point to help her with all the arrangements for the funeral and anything else she needs and Mary thanks Frankie for all his support.

It is so difficult for Frankie to be in the house with Mary surrounded by so many reminders of Davey, the photographs, 'Davey's chair', so many memories. Seeing the kids so upset and Mary is so tiny and fragile, Frankie worries dreadfully for her. But he has to go as he has other promises to keep.

Frankie then drives Donna, Tony and Rosie up to see me in hospital. By the time they get here, I am in a much better condition and almost back to my best, I've had a blood transfusion and the medication has broken the fever that I had succumbed to due to the infection.

Donna hugs me with all her strength and I feel a lucky man, Rosie holds my hand and doesn't let go and Tony just says well done boss man to me, although Razor sees the deep concern in his eyes. He later tells me that Frankie did tell them about my heroics and that he might have even embellished the story a little bit more, but I wasn't going to deny a thing.

We are spoken to the by the Police separately and together and our stories seem to tally and they seemed happy enough to believe the part we played in everything that happened on the mountain. It was clear that the Police saw how devastating that the events had been to both of us, losing our friends and someone we had only just met wasn't part of our plans and in such a senseless way.

Frankie, Donna, Tony and Rosie stay in a local Bed and breakfast that Frankie has sorted. The next day, Frankie drives us all back home to Glasgow in the rental that he hired as his four by four is still up at the cabin. We all get home and Donna and the kids say goodbye to Frankie, we hug each other tight and hold the embrace for a long time, both men have tears in their eyes as they separate.

We both understood how close they came to death and escaping with our lives is just the start of the healing process, we have a lot of guilt to overcome and that may take some time yet

The Police are regular visitors to both of us over the few weeks leading up to the funerals and some of the things they tell us about Jack are unbelievable. The fact that we saw him regularly and didn't know what he was going through was disastrous for us as friends and we paid the ultimate price for it. To be fair to us, he did hide it well.

Jack had created a whole alter ego for 'Bobby', completely separating Jack's actions from Bobby's actions and vice versa. It seems that Jack put all his weaker characteristics onto Bobby, but made out that it was Bobby who was the I.T. specialist and Jack had created a complete life for himself with a wife and three kids and a job as a mechanic and a house in the suburbs. The Police told us that Jack had recorded all of our lives on his computers and hard drives and if they hadn't been through so much already, they might have delved deeper into our lives.

As it was, they were quite ready to overlook some of the misdemeanours that may have occurred, but that if they were to call by one day unannounced and find any cannabis or other drugs in or around the house 'Mr McGregor', they may have to act on it.

Me and Donna took the hint and to be honest and thinking about kids, the decision was made easier to pack in the weed anyway. But one of the strangest things that came out was that Jack had split his Last Will and Testament between his three best friends, David Donnelly, Francis McMullen and Paul McGregor. Both of us are completely shell shocked as we know Jack could have potentially been a millionaire, but that's with legal teams of one sort or another and they don't really care too much for the money right now anyway.

The week before Davey's funeral, Frankie drove the two of us up to Lossiemouth for the funeral of Robert Page, the Ranger. The vicar talks well of Robert, a local boy who was always outdoors as a young child, enjoying nature and wildlife which led him to his role as a Parks Ranger which he was so proud of when he got the job. He paid the ultimate sacrifice for his work and died a well-loved man. We are both devastated for Robert's parents at losing their only son. It is difficult for us to speak to them as we feel some sort of responsibility for what happened for his death.

Fortunately for us, the family see our anxiety and reassure us that they feel no malice towards us for what happened and they understand that there was nothing that we could have done. They also tell us they are very sorry for our own loss, losing close friends is just like losing family they tell us.

The family spoke to me and Frankie for a long time after the funeral, thanking us for attending and asking us about Robert's last hours. We were honest in our opinion of him in that although we didn't know him well, he seemed a lovely guy who had a great sense of humour and spoke of his home town with affection. I did throw in that he hated the RAF and all those bloody English and this raised a smile to all those within hearing distance.

We left Lossiemouth having completed one of the three funerals that we had to attend with a sense of relief. The funeral had been a nice one, very subdued and respectful but with lots of happiness for a young man who had been well liked and respected by family, friends and townsfolk.

Davey's funeral was on the Friday and the Tuesday before was Jack's. We were apprehensive about attending Jack's funeral, we tried to explain to Mary why we were attending, about how we felt some responsibility for Jack's state of mind and that however we were feeling about what he had done to Davey and the Ranger, he had been a friend for so long and he was still our friend.

We told her what the Police had told us, particularly that he was in great pain in trying to deal with his issues. Mary said she accepted what we were saying, but that she would never, ever forgive Jack for what he had done. We told her that we accepted what she had said but we felt that we owed it to Jack to go.

There had been quite a clamour for a story both locally and nationally when the story broke, but they weren't going to get anything from us. The bigger stations and publications accepted our request for privacy, but the gutter press and paparazzi wouldn't leave us in peace even when one of them got a good pasting from another friend of ours. Funny enough, the Police weren't interested in pressing charges.

The weather was horrid on the day of Jack's funeral. Grey and leaden sky took all the colour out of the day and the rain fell in a deluge in straight lines from the heavy clouds flooding roads and footpaths, streets were empty and it was just a bloody miserable day all round. It rained all through the funeral and there were only a few attendees which made the occasion even sadder.

His uncle who owned the cabin, Peter turned up. He muttered some apologies and condolences our way, my injuries are not visible, but Frankie's scar is a shocker and I think he was more embarrassed to be there. There were a few 'geeky' looking individuals who had turned up who I assumed knew Jack in some cyber world or other.

There were also some reporters outside the crematorium when we came in and Frankie told them they best not be there when we come out. They weren't, Frankie looks quite fearsome with the scar and a growl.

The vicar mumbled through the service until I couldn't bear it any longer and I stood up and asked if he would mind if I said a few words. He looked quite relieved to be honest.

I spoke out to the half a dozen people who were there and told them about all Jack's good points, how successful he had been as a businessman, how we had known each other from young boys at school and how he always supported us all through the tough times in our lives.

I let them know that he was our friend and we should have been there for him more and been able to help him with his mental health problems, but we weren't and that makes us all a little sorrier and feeling a little empty as a result. My voice trails off after saying this and I hang my head somewhat in shame, tears running freely down my face.

I hear a shuffle of feet and Frankie comes to help me back to my seat while the vicar says a final prayer and we walk out into the rain with Weller's 'Black is the Colour' playing us out. We thought it appropriate.

♦ ♦ ♦ ♦ ♦ ♦

As we stand at the graveside with our families around us and Mary and the boys in our protective circle, tears flow and handkerchiefs are passed around. There is a great turn out because as big and scary as Davey was, he was also fiercely loyal to anyone who was honest with him.

As the priest says the final few words and utters the immortal 'ashes to ashes, dust to dust', we all follow Mary and the boys in dropping soil onto the lid of Davey's coffin. I hear Frankie whisper 'God bless big man' and I follow suit with 'we will never forget you big Davey', being careful that the catch in my throat doesn't turn into a sob.

As we turn away from the grave, the sound of crying is heard all around the grave site and I find it difficult to hold back my own tears. Just then a voice calls out 'Excuse me gents, can I have a word?'

Me and Frankie turn around and there is an old guy in a black suit and tie and a long black overcoat, he is with a young man who we recognise right away, it is the 'businessman' who broke

Davey's bones and he is with his son. He must see the look of shock on our faces and it dawns on us who he is. We tell the women and kids to go to the cars and we'll follow on.

'Relax boys, I'm just here to pay my respects. You're pal was an honest guy who I had a lot of time for after he took his punishment. He was like one of the old time brawlers, but this new world of drugs, gangs and guns just wasn't for him.' He pauses and looks out across the cemetery before carrying on.

'Anyway, I'm very sorry for your loss boys and if there is anything you need or particularly Mrs Donnelly, please give me a call.' And with that, his son passes Frankie a business card and they both turn away heading to the exit of the cemetery. Me and Frankie both look at each other and almost laugh at what has just happened, we think Davey might have had a bit of a chuckle about that as well.

After the funeral, we head back to Mary's house. It feels strange to call it that, we've always said we will meet at Davey's house or Davey's pad or whatever, it was never Mary's house. Most of the people from the funeral head back there too and they all shake Mary by the hand and share their own personal tales with her of the big man.

It's quite difficult to make it a celebration of Davey's life as the pain is too raw and the fact that it was Jack who killed him and he was one of our own is just too difficult to comprehend right now. Everyone leaves by about ten o'clock except for me, Frankie and Donna, Davey's boys are up in their rooms playing some computer game or other. We all give a hand straightening up the house and getting most of the dishes washed and dried and then we all grab a drink and head to the living room.

We sit in a comfortable silence, just sharing the feeling of Davey and Mary's home and look at the pictures of their family together taken over a number of years.

'He was a great man.' Mary says, 'A great man, a great father and a great husband and I am going to miss him so much.' Mary breaks down at this point and Donna gets up and goes over to Mary and pulls her into her embrace.

'Aye he was Mary, a really great man, a great husband and the best of friends.' Frankie says. 'And you're right Mary, it will be hard to get over him, I doubt you ever will, none of us will. But we will all be here for you and for each other and we will get through this, together.'

'Aye,' I say, 'Aye we will.'

## Author's Note

Having visited Scotland only a couple of times and this was only to Glasgow and Edinburgh, I have used my literary license, imagination and no too small amount of time on Google Earth© to fill in the details that were not at my disposal. I would seek forgiveness for any errors in my descriptions as I have the utmost respect for my friends from the North. But what a journey it was, travelling along roads, passing mountains, lochs, forests and glens, Scotland is truly a magical place and I plan to visit at the next available opportunity.

The journey to the mountain was as accurate as I could make it, unfortunately, the mountain is fictitious. I had to make it out of the way as possible for the remoteness and as high as possible without eclipsing Ben Nevis.

I really enjoyed writing this book, not only for the scenery but for the camaraderie and friendship of the group of friends, it was only a shame I had to kill some of them off!

On a more serious note, mental health and mental wellbeing are things that affect each and every one of us and it is important to be aware of some of the issues that can impact on individuals on a daily basis. There are support systems out there, but the pressure on these services is immense and they struggle to cope with the volume of referrals that they receive.

I have been working on a mental health project as part of my day job recently and there are a number of tools and techniques available to individuals such as mindfulness that may help if you or someone you know is struggling to cope with poor mental wellbeing. More information about this and other support services can be found at www.mind.org.uk.

## About the Author

Tommy Dunn was born in Liverpool, UK, in 1970 and lived with his parents, two brothers and one sister. He still lives in the City with his wife Nicola and two of his three children, his eldest child having recently had her own baby, making him Grandad Tommy!

This is the second piece of work from the author, his first, 'Another Life' is a novella which has had rave online reviews.

Tommy is currently working on his third novel, 'A Murder of Innocents', a dark story of a serial child killer and the detective assigned to solve the case. It promises to be a full blooded affair with twists and turns throughout, keep a look for future titles coming out in 2017.

## Don't forget

Thanks so much for purchasing THE BEST OF FRIENDS and I really hope you enjoyed the read. Grab your bonus, please visit my website www.thomasdunnauthor.com to pick up my **free** novella ANOTHER LIFE. By signing up I agree not to bombard you with spam as some other unscrupulous individuals will do, just information about progress on my writing and new book releases.

Printed in Great Britain
by Amazon